Robert James Oliver, or 'Bob' as he is known to friends and family, was born in Greenock, Scotland, to a Scottish mother and an English father.

Back in 1956, his mother wanted him and his elder sister, Maggie, who was three years old at the time, to grow up in Scotland, but his father insisted on his family being with him in his hometown of Canterbury, Kent.

He had a good job at the time – a boiler engineer in the city's hospital shovelling coal for eight-hour shifts, which was better than he could get in Scotland back in those bleak days.

After six months of tense negotiations – mainly by letter – Bob's father executed a rescue mission and brought his family back to Kent, where they would grow up with English accents and the memories of a council estate that would inspire not only Bob but his now four sisters to get out and 'find a better place'.

If you ever question Bob about whose side he is on when England plays Scotland at any type of sport, he will reply, "My head is with England, but my heart is always with Scotland."

Bob now lives in Farnborough, Hampshire, along with his beloved wife and daughter.

To Jacob Stapleton, the 'giant king of IT' who has made all of this possible.

To the amazing Marcus Malone who actually does exist and can be found on YouTube/iTunes singing the very songs I mention in this book – thanks so much, big guy!

Also to my dear friend Daniel Card who has watched this story evolve from a little baby in 2006 to the monster teenager that it is now – father and granddaddy coming soon.

Robert James Oliver

THE WOLF

AUSTIN MACAULEY PUBLISHERS™
LONDON • CAMBRIDGE • NEW YORK • SHARJAH

Copyright © Robert James Oliver (2021)

The right of Robert James Oliver to be identified as author of this work has been asserted by the author in accordance with section 77 and 78 of the Copyright, Designs and Patents Act 1988.

All rights reserved. No part of this publication may be reproduced, stored in a retrieval system, or transmitted in any form or by any means, electronic, mechanical, photocopying, recording, or otherwise, without the prior permission of the publishers.

Any person who commits any unauthorised act in relation to this publication may be liable to criminal prosecution and civil claims for damages.

This is a work of fiction. Names, characters, businesses, places, events, locales, and incidents are either the products of the author's imagination or used in a fictitious manner. Any resemblance to actual persons, living or dead, or actual events is purely coincidental.

A CIP catalogue record for this title is available from the British Library.

ISBN 9781528977432 (Paperback)
ISBN 9781528977456 (ePub e-book)

www.austinmacauley.com

First Published (2021)
Austin Macauley Publishers Ltd
25 Canada Square
Canary Wharf
London
E14 5LQ

To Desmond Bagley – author of *The Naked Ape*. During an interview, he was asked if he could remove one human ability, what would it be? He replied, "I would remove the power of speech – there has to be a better way of communicating with each other."

My wonderful friend Tom Branagh – *Burnt Out Bikes* – rule the New Forest! Thanks for the info, buddy.

The she-wolf watched as her pack leader lifted his nose high into the air, every sense straining to pinpoint the danger.

They all knew what it was, humans, and even worse, humans with dogs.

She loathed both of these filthy, uncivilised creatures with all of her soul and at first light, distant sounds and distant smells of these monsters were brought in on the early morning breeze.

The twenty strong pack were camped deep in a snow-covered forest, somewhere in St Victor Provincial Park, Canada, close to the border with America, probably too close.

They had been hidden away from the outside world but someone or something had found them and they were now being hunted down.

They had prospered during the summer, uninterrupted by the outside world but with winter approaching, their whole world suddenly looked very cold.

Earlier on, the pack leader and his two subordinates had forced the whole gang to move quickly. The smell of human and dog followed them as they ran for an hour without rest, and now they were at a crossroads, the edge of the forest. In front of them a clear area of land, then a tree covered landscape that might provide escape – Wood Mountain.

The leader had to decide the next move and all eyes were laid upon him.

The she-wolf looked down as her two young cubs nudged against her for reassurance and she reciprocated with a motherly touch.

The sound of barking dogs someway off sent the pack into a near panic but then the leader calmed them with a vicious growl.

A few tense seconds passed before he made the final decision.

They would 'run'. They had to, there was nowhere else to go.

The she-wolf held back, sensing more danger on the open plain, but by now it was too late – the leader sprinted towards the mountain and the whole pack followed, apart from her.

The cubs followed the throng only pausing for a second to look back at their howling mother. Torn between duty and mother, they chose duty.

"Come back my beloved ones," she screamed.

The nearly entire pack had only been on the open ground for a few moments before shots rang out. The leader was the first to go down, followed by his trusted lieutenants and then the systematic slaughter of all she held dear, began.

The mindset of the pack was to follow, only she had remained. None of them came back.

Her blood turned cold as her survival instinct went into overdrive.

The dogs were getting closer, she would let them come. Slinking back into the undergrowth, she hid herself as well as she could, moving slowly toward the oncoming threat.

Hiding within some thick bushes she remained as still as possible. The dogs now sensed wolf blood.

"They will pass me by without a thought but their own want; such a stupid race."

Dogs and humans passed by her hiding place, many of them. When she sensed safety, she moved on, retracing the snow labelled footsteps of the pack.

She increased her speed thinking all danger was now behind her, not quite.

Suddenly she came face to face with a human who appeared to be amazed to see her there. The wolf's eyes turned blood-red and charged at the creature.

The next thing she felt was the burning sensation of a bullet that drilled a narrow furrow across her left shoulder even before she'd heard the sound of the shot. It spun her around and down on her haunches; she suffered a split second of shock before her instincts once again took over. Licking quickly at the new wound, she raised herself up.

The next sound she heard was a 'click'.

The human in front of her was desperately trying to reload a weapon.

"Take a deep breath, beast, for on all this earth, it will certainly be your last."

She ran at full speed toward the creature and leapt into the air.

Just before she clamped her jaws around her victim's throat, she noticed a pair of bright blue eyes and long blond hair.

"A she-human, this has such soft skin."

The weight of the wriggling angry wolf tore the entire throat from the woman and she dropped to the ground.

A thought came to the wolf as she witnessed the final death throes of the animal in front of her – the mountain. Somehow, she must cross over the open ground if she were to survive. The thoughts of her pack leader and father of her two sons came back to her. There really was nowhere else to go.

"One must turn back to go forward, whatever awaits, if indeed it waits, may be better than before."

She turned back toward her family's carnage and applied the same tactics as before, creeping and hiding through the forest, back towards the open space that would determine life or death.

The humans and dogs were victorious. She could hear the shouts and barks of celebration.

They must have ignored the one gunshot that ploughed a bloody groove through her shoulder due to the executions of her wounded family members.

Reaching the edge of the forest again, she watched from under cover as the humans piled her entire pack into one heap. Men appeared from the snow, 'dressed as snow', carrying weapons.

She looked at these alien figures and wondered in disgust at the horrific world that she was in.

"Men in the snow, dressed as snow?"

Pieces of her family were given to the dogs, the heart of the pack leader amongst other items and the humans drank merrily from small silver hip flasks.

Suddenly all was not well with them, shouts went up, cries of disbelief, shouts of, "Helga! Helga!"

Most importantly for her, every human and every dog ran back into the forest.

She took the opportunity and ran like she'd never run before, across the open ground toward the foot of Wood Mountain.

She reached relative safety before the first shots rang out. They appeared distant and she knew safety had been achieved.

Turning and facing her foe in defiance, she finally chewed and swallowed the propensities taken from her victim.

She felt no pain from her wound, that would come later.

***

At the top of the mountain, the she-wolf finally stopped running.

She sniffed at the air, all was clear. She knew that they would be coming for her but for now she was safe. Laying down in the snow she sensed a sudden change in temperature. The wind was changing; it would become very cold soon. In normal circumstances, the pack would huddle together. But now there was just her. She thought long and hard about her situation before raising her head, listening to the world and what it had to offer her. A call came, it was a cry for help or something, as she turned to face south – her mind raced, strategy, reason, action. The destination and purpose became clear, logical in fact. She laid down once more, resting, confirming her analogy.

"Future is nothing more than change; you cannot change the future, you can only change yourself."

Her tongue hung outside the long pointed and toothy snout as she panted. Controlling her anger, she put the recent past inside a locked memory deep in her mind and then was up and running once more, running fast down the mountain side heading south.

She ran downhill without pause for the rest of that day, homing in on the mysterious cry for help; she was getting closer. Another mile or so down the mountain side, she finally found the source. The tracks were human, footprints and a large furrow in the snow like something large was being dragged. A blood trail coated the ploughed snow; she licked at the pink liquid, still fresh.

A discarded weapon lay in the snow and she sniffed at the item undisturbed; they were only frightening in the hands of humans.

She slowed now, treading cautiously, following the bloody groove as it made its way downhill.

On she went, further down the gentle slope until suddenly the reason for the trail of blood appeared. Immediately she took cover off the rough track and surveyed the confused scene.

She looked down to a large dead elk that had been shot in the chest. The red blood still oozed profusely from the newly created hole.

The animal laid on its side, its two hind legs bound by a thick rope which stretched out to a man who was struggling to pull the creature further down the mountain. He pulled his last effort before giving up completely.

The man let out a last moan and collapsed in the snow; he attempted to stand up but could only barely manage a kneeling position. The sudden change in weather had caught him unaware and unprepared.

The wolf watched in fascination as he managed to pull a packet of cigarettes from the top pocket of his thin jacket, he only succeeded in spilling the entire contents onto the snow. His frozen fingers picked up one small cigarette and put it to his shaking mouth. She looked on impassively at the man's determined effort to light the smoke. He probably had the only Zippo in the world at that time that would 'not' light.

Giving up, he fell onto his side thrusting his frozen hands underneath his armpits, and curling his knees up to his waist.

The wolf ran swiftly to the dead elk. She had not eaten for three days, apart from the human's throat and now gorged on the dead animal ripping out the entrails from the soft belly.

After filling her stomach, she rested for a while and looked at the man curled up in a death pose. Something interested her; she didn't know what it was, just a sense of daring maybe, which did not suit her character at all.

Slowly she approached the forlorn figure. She knew there was no danger from this human and the feeling was certainly not pity. Still, curiosity drove her closer.

Standing over him she noticed faint signs of life, little breaths of steam escaped from his mouth. She sniffed at this and he curled up even tighter. At this she backed off sharply.

After a few moments, she approached once more and started pawing at the man who could only moan softly. Now just little sniffs exhaled from his nostrils as he struggled to even breath. It was getting late in the day at this point, darkness was beginning to approach and she felt very tired. Suddenly, the need to sleep became overpowering.

Against all her natural instincts and ignoring the strange smell of this creature, she laid herself on top of him.

He didn't respond, which eased her worry and began fussing around to find a comfortable position until she eventually calmed and began to sleep.

The snow then fell heavily, covering both wolf and man.

***

The unlikely couple awoke at the first light of day, covered with a thick layer of snow. Thankfully the icy wind had abated. The air was still, but cold all the same.

During the night, the man had battled to stay alive. The wolf was big, but not sizable enough to cover all of his body, even though he was just a small skinny guy. His legs from the knee down were the most exposed but luckily, the only decent bit of clothing he wore were a pair of thick socks inside a brand-new pair of sturdy boots.

Even so, his own personal sacrifice for life was going to be the loss of at least a couple of toes. Both his hands were still thrust under opposite armpits; they were the lucky ones. The living blanket of wolf would be his saviour.

After an hour or so of thick snowfall, they had become fairly well insulated. Due to his sparse and cheap clothing however, he was wet in places. Instinct told him that if the wolf left him, he would freeze to death in minutes. With this in mind he had stayed awake for most of the night, with the damp comforting smell of the animal filling his nostrils and her deep sounding snores filling his ears. It was one of those situations where life and death was held in the balance between the tiniest of decisions.

He awoke in agony as the wolf suddenly got up, causing him to whimper.

The communal warmth built between them disappeared in an instant.

She too awoke with a yelp from the pain in her left shoulder and limped towards the dead elk now covered in snow.

She gorged once more on this feast, which by now was frozen stiff, occasionally glancing up at the man's pathetic attempts to stand up. He seemed to be losing the battle. Deciding to take action, she paused her meal and approached the pathetic creature. Blood-covered jaws growled next to his face, her eyes, red with anger – the message to the man was clear.

"If you continue to die man-human, I will wait upon that moment when your heart ceases to beat and then eat your still warm flesh, possibly even before such a time."

To sanction this thought, she snapped at the man's thigh, drawing blood, then she grasped the bottom of his jeans and shook her head like a mad dog. This action pumped the last remaining drops of adrenalin into the man's system and he somehow got to his feet. Satisfied, the wolf returned to her feast of elk meat.

The man staggered downhill toward where he knew his old pickup truck was parked, less than one mile away.

He glanced back to the wolf as she ripped into the carcass of the beast that he had shot and dragged downhill for almost a mile the day before.

It would have provided meat for him for months but now his only concern was the next 30 minutes or so. His truck was only a half mile away now – just get the engine running

– hopefully, the flask of soup that he had brought along was still a little warm.

By the time he reached his vehicle, his desperation was such that he had completely forgotten about the wolf. Elation at finding the vehicle had taken away all his fear. As his frozen hand struggled with the key however, it suddenly returned. The lock clicked open but then this comforting sound was followed by a blood curdling growl from behind him.

She stood, ten feet away from him, teeth-stripped and ready to pounce.

They eyeballed each other for what seemed like minutes. It seemed that she was verbally assaulting him until he finally gave in and lent back against the side of the vehicle, arms lowered, awaiting the inevitable attack.

This never came but the standoff continued until the man in desperation and more than a little bit of fascination blurted out.

"What exactly do you want from me, wolf?"

She suddenly stopped her threats at this comment. "Much more than you will ever know, human."

She calmed and carefully edged towards the man, keeping close eye contact as she moved. His hand still held the door handle. The wolf gently muzzled at it still staring into his eyes, hypnotising him. She then backed off a few feet and sat down in the snow. "Mmmmrr," she growled gently.

With a piece of his remaining strength, he grabbed at the handle and pulled the door fully open whilst still leaning against the side of the pickup.

The wolf leapt past him, over the driver's side and settled down on the double passenger seat, pawing and scratching at the cloth upholstery. Finally, she made herself comfortable and began licking her still weeping wound.

The man struggled into the driver's seat and with a quick prayer to God, turned the key. The engine burst into life first time, an answer to his prayer. She watched as his still frozen fingers managed to take the top from a silver flask. An unfamiliar odour filled the cab – tomato soup. He went to offer her some of it but she declined and continued to stare at him before rising up on all four legs, appearing to be sick. Her stomach convulsed as she coughed up a large piece of the recently eaten elk. It lay steaming on the edge of the seat.

The man took up the pink steak and tore at it greedily. He too had not eaten for some time. He then offered what was left back to the wolf. She once again declined so he scooped the rest of the pink mush into the cup of the flask and patted it down.

"We'll save that for later eh, boy?"

"Eat it all, you require it."

The wolf rested on all fours once again but still looked on impassively.

He waited for a full five minutes before turning on the heater's blower.

Wonderful, wonderful warm air filled the cab, causing the windows to steam up. As the man thawed in the now sauna-like conditions, his mind went back to a cage in Vietnam. A time past, when his life had also been threatened. So much pain, so much hardship, but he had survived – in solitude, he had survived. Now he was half dead through cold and sharing a small space with a large, menacing and angry wolf.

"How strange is that?" he laughed and mumbled to himself.

Putting the truck into gear, he took another glance at his new companion who was enjoying the heat so much she rolled onto her back favouring her bad side and stretched her legs in the air.

"Hey, look at you, I see you ain't no 'boy' either," he observed.

Her eyes opened and closed in apparent answer to this statement. He also noticed the flecks of beige hair on her head and body; she was a northern grey wolf. Although he was no expert in wolves, he just thought that she looked absolutely beautiful.

"You have a gunshot wound. I guess you must be in a heap of trouble, wolf?"

The man lifted his hand to inspect the injured shoulder of the wolf but she growled loudly at this action.

"Get away from me beast; your kind revolts me."

Pulling his hand back quickly, he raised the clutch of his pick up to move the vehicle forward and down the basic track from where he'd begun his 'mission' a day before.

"Well, I can fix that up if you want, just let me know, eh?"

The wolf growled gently in acknowledgement and then closed her eyes to sleep.

The man headed down the rugged mountain track that would lead him home, which was over 2,000 miles away.

During the war, his best friend had told him about shooting elk in Canada.

"See if you get to shoot one of these guys, you get food for a year! As long as you don't mind eating elk meat every day!"

The pain in his feet reminded him of what his friend had also said about the sudden changes in temperature that can happen in the Canadian mountains.

They had only gone about a mile down the mountain before he looked down at his new companion whose eyelids were moving franticly. "Bad dream, eh wolf?"

Then they opened and the man read fear in her eyes as she began to growl loudly. He had seen this before from an old colleague who had a natural sense of danger, and now he was picking up on this same action from a wolf that he barely knew.

Something threatening was out there. As far as he was aware, they were the only living souls for miles around, but now he also sensed 'danger'.

"OK, wolf, I get it."

The man stopped there and then. Reaching underneath the dashboard, he pulled out a very small pair of army-issued binoculars.

Leaving the truck quickly and shutting the door on the now frantic wolf, he hobbled up to the highest point that he could find and surveyed the area. He remembered the road that wound around the mountain and focused on whatever part he could see. All clear up to where he was but a fleck of movement in the distance caught his well-trained eye.

Three specs moving at speed, heading towards him and it had to be his way, there was no other way.

"Oh, looky here, wolf, you were correct; we are going to have company."

He limped quickly back to the truck to find the wolf holding a large piece of the seat fabric in her mouth and madly staring at him through the truck window.

"Aw man did you have to do that?"

He beckoned her to calm down and move back to her own side. To his surprise, she obeyed this request and he got back into his driver's seat looking at her mad, angry face and wondering if he had done the right thing.

The narrow track would only facilitate one vehicle but there were passing points along the way.

Noticing a small lay-up and a ditch on his left, he carefully put his driver side wheel into the depression so that the old tank would look abandoned.

The wolf began to slide down the double seats as the truck went into an incline. The man thought twice about putting his hand out to stop her landing on him but she sensed this and bit into the door handle to steady herself, which caused half of the door panel to begin coming away.

"Yea go on wolf, wreck my ride."

He looked to the wolf who was starting to feel the pain of the previous 36 hours and looked in a bad way. Suddenly he felt a feeling of compassion, a rare feeling that he hadn't experienced in years or perhaps ever before.

"You stay there, girl."

Struggling to walk on his bad feet, the man grabbed a shovel from the back of his truck and began moving snow onto the outside wheels and windscreen to make it look as though the vehicle had been there for some time.

He had used this ruse before with sand and he hoped it would work again with snow.

Looking through the passenger door window he stared straight into the blood-red eyes of the wolf, who was getting very angry again.

"Shhhsssh." The man ordered, putting one finger up to his lips, and surprisingly she agreed with him. She calmed and laid back down across the seat, still at an incline.

They both heard it together, the distant sound of engines, coming towards them.

Hurriedly rubbing away his footprints with a branch, the man went around to the driver's door and beckoned the wolf out of his truck before shutting the door. She knew instantly the oncoming danger and ran to the cover of a nearby copse.

He wiped out her tracks and his with the same branch.

They hid side by side as the three all-terrain vehicles roared past them; only the last one paused briefly to check out the man's old pickup truck.

From his hidden position, he noticed the men sitting in the open back of the vehicle and the weapons they carried before it moved on. She sat and sniffed, calculating and remembering everything that had gone before her.

As the three ATVs disappeared up the snow filled track, they eyed each other – both questioning – both trusting – both asking, when do we move?

First one eyebrow – then one lick of vicious teeth – a shrug of shoulders – followed by a sniff into the air. Good to go!

They both ran to the truck, her limping and favouring her left side and him comically hobbling along as if walking on hot coals.

As an afterthought, he limped back to their hiding place with the broken branch and attempted to rub out all traces of them having been there. She grabbed the door handle with her teeth and opened the door before leaping inside and grabbing hold of the broken passenger door handle to lay herself on the inclined seat.

The man quickly followed and naturally sat in the driver's seat to turn on the ignition.

The truck's engine roared into life and reversed effortlessly out of the ditch, then downwards towards the border road as fast as the old piece of junk would go.

***

The three ATVs sped up the mountain track past the 'ditched' pickup truck and reached the point that they could go no further. In the far distance, the sound of dogs barking excitedly filled the air.

The leader of the party ordered everyone to, "look for the wolf! Find the tracks, find the tracks!" 15 men ran from the vehicles and desperately searched for clues in the snow. They found some in the track that led down to where they were and everyone converged on that point.

A short while later two Native American Chippewa Indians who had tracked the she-wolf all day and night arrived. Their dogs could still be heard in the distance but after a while they became silent; just the men walked down to the area.

The leader stood to greet them.

"Where is the wolf?" he asked.

One of the Chippewa Indian guides surveyed the scene up and down before answering.

"We followed the tracks to here, but then you and your men have just walked across everything since then, so we don't know where it is."

The leader, was 'Hans Schnell', a retired police detective who along with his wife 'Helga' ran a gun school just outside of Geneva, Switzerland. He also organised international 'shooting parties' for exclusive clients who would pay thousands of dollars for the thrill of killing exotic animals.

This particular shoot had been sanctioned by the Canadian government.

It was to 'cull' a small pack of wolves that had evolved too close to the American border. His 'clients' now shocked by the death of his wife wanted to return to their hotel and then back to Switzerland as soon as they could. Hans Schnell just wanted to find the wolf. Ironically his wife had not wanted to join in with the actual 'cull', so the husband had joked about only giving her a single shot weapon. She should have been safe with the Native American Indian guides, who were employed by the Canadian Forestry Commission but maybe she had got lost in all the confusion.

The plan had been simple. The dogs would force the pack out of the forest and onto the open ground with the only feasible escape route being Wood Mountain.

Carefully disguised shooting pits had been created with a safely angled crossfire in mind; once on the open ground, the pack would have stood no chance at all.

Mr Schnell ceased to be in control of himself or the situation. He just knelt down in the snow and cried for the loss of his wife…

After letting the man mourn for a short time, one of the 'Chippewa' guides approached him as he wept in the snow.

"There was a man here, he left this."

Hans Schnell stopped crying and stood up to look at the rifle offered to him. His professional eye immediately noticed an anomaly.

"M16A1, standard issue, but the carrying handle has been taken off to accommodate a huge set of Russian telescopic sights, Dragunov for sure, PSO1. I am confused. What sort of weapon is this? Is it for a sniper? Have you seen this before?"

"Check it out," replied the Chippewa as he handed the gun to Hans Scnhell, who took hold of the unique weapon and after a few minutes, managed to unlock the huge sights from its bracket-like holder, fixed with four butterfly nuts to one side of the M16A1. It was a strange configuration. He looked through the sights and was amazed at their clarity, at long distance. He had heard of 'Dragunov' telescopic sights before but had never experienced their performance.

Hans Schnell couldn't understand the reason why the best Russian sights in the world had been attached to a common American assault weapon. "Who would have used this?"

"Vietnam War weapon, not a sniper. M16s nowhere good enough. Not regular GIs either; they didn't have a choice of weapons so, maybe an infiltration force or 'snatch squad' as we called them, special forces; those guys went behind enemy lines to capture Cong members for interrogation, and I'm not talking about enlisted men. They kidnapped hard-core people and they did have their choice of weapons, but this looks like some sort of experimental hybrid built by a 'gun freak on acid'. These sights however would give you the best eyes, better than anything we had so anyhow, that would be my guess."

One of the Chippewa Indians explained, he and his 'brother' partner were ex-Vietnam veterans themselves.

"That would have been a dangerous mission?" Hans Schnell asked looking through the sights again being amazed at their range and clarity.

"Oh yea, they were pretty out there."

"Why has such a man been here and where is he now?"

"He was shooting elk; there's a dead one a little way back up the hill there, and he also left this."

The Indian guide handed Hans Schnell a Zippo lighter. His hand gently rubbed over the hand inscribed initials, H.W.

"How would he even get here?"

"Well, he would not have walked here. There was talk of guy that used to come here all the time, but not for the last year or so, by all accounts – he used to come in an old pickup truck and park it right here."

"A truck!!! There was an abandoned truck on the way up to this point?"

"It wasn't there two days ago," the Chippewa Indian informed him.

Hans Schnell grabbed the Indian and the two of them sped back down the mountain trail until they reached the point where the man had laid up his flatbed truck. Hans began to get out of the ATV but the Indian stopped him.

"Stay here, let me look around."

The man had made a good job of covering up the tracks of the wolf but this was a professional tracker; it only took half a paw print in the snow to confirm that the wolf had been there.

The Chippewa returned to the ATV and reported to Hans Schnell.

"They were here, and now they are (looking at his watch) crossing the border, probably at East Poplar."

Hans Schnell looked at the man in desperation, knowing that without the relevant visa, he could not follow.

***

Hunter Wisekat was having the ride of his life. Pushing a beaten up, old flatbed truck down the side of a mountain as fast as it would go.

"Hey, wolf!" he shouted. She got half up, but the pain of her wound made her fall back onto the seat of the bouncing truck.

This was followed by cackles of mad laughter from Hunter.

"Boy, aren't we having fun now, eh girl?"

She answered him by clamping her jaws albeit gently around his right elbow so that every time the vehicle hit a bump, he would receive a small nip from her sharp teeth.

Hunter got the message and slowed instantly.

"OK, OK, just let me go there, wolf."

"I am not enjoying this strange human world"

Twenty minutes later, they reached the Canadian/American border.

His friend had told him the exact border crossing to use.

'American friendly – foreign aggressive'

Hunter took his passport from the glove compartment and proceeded to cover the wolf with a blanket and some coats so that just her head was exposed. With her unique colouring, he was convinced that she would pass for a husky dog. Bravely, he whispered in her ear, "For the next few minutes, you are a dog."

Somehow, she managed to control her inner anger.

"Is this my future? Am I to become a dog?"

Hunter drove the old truck up to the check point.

Inside the main office, an older border guard noticed the vehicle arrive and relieved one of the younger men under his supervision.

Approaching Hunter, he had a slight bemused look on his face.

"Can I see your passport, sir?" he spoke through the passenger door window that Hunter had reached over and opened.

To Hunter's amazement, the wolf remained still as the guard reached over her to grasp his document.

The border guard studied his passport intently and for some reason unknown to him asked,

"You were in Nam?"

It was more an answer than a question.

"Uhah," Hunter answered guardedly.

The border guard smiled knowingly.

"Been shooting elk? I see you haven't got none."

"No, sir! No elk on this trip."

"Well, that's a first; see I've seen this old jalopy carry many a feast back to the world. So how come you got the mission, your friend not up to it anymore?"

"No, sir! He died."

The guard looked distant and sad for a moment.

"I'm very sorry to hear that. I just have to ask you one more question, sir. Do you have any weapons with you?"

This caused a tear to well in Hunter's eye, pangs of guilt attacked him as he recalled the moment that he'd thrown away his best friend's prized possession to save his own life – a rare M16A1 fitted with huge Russian Dragunov sights.

Hunter's personal weapon was an AK47 hidden away at his desert farm in Arizona. He did, however have his own army-issued M16 hidden underneath the old pickup along with ammunition.

"No, sir! I do not."

The guard looked Hunter straight in the eye and believed him but then looked a little closer at the wolf.

"I can tell on this occasion you have had a bad trip, sir. I mean, just look at you and your dog; you both look all beat up, and hey, that is a dog. Isn't it?"

"It sure is."

The border guard thought long and hard before asking.

"You been driving the sled a bit hard, maybe?"

"No, sir! She is just a lazy bitch," Hunter answered quickly.

The wolf looked quickly to the guard, then Hunter and then down, trying so hard to contain her anger before emitting a tiny, "Woof, woof" sound.

The border guard smiled, satisfied and announced. "Good doggy, you take care of your owner there; he's a good man," and went to pat the wolf on her wounded shoulder.

Hunter leant over and grabbed the guard's hand in a flash.

"I'm sorry, sir! She doesn't like being touched."

Looking directly into Hunter's eyes, the border guard slowly relinquished and took a step back.

"I understand. OK, sir! You are free to pass."

Handing back Hunter's passport, the guard took one step back and stood to attention before announcing loudly.

"Welcome back to America!"

***

Hunter and the wolf crossed the border and drove on for a few hours before he spoke again.

"I'm sorry. I just had to say all that stuff."

The she-wolf glared at the man.

"Even though I detest you, human, your functions are familiar to me, your thoughts and words are understandable, your odour is bearable and most of all, for now...you are all that I have."

Hunter drove on deep into North Dakota. He did have a plan that was now changing by the second. He should have been carrying 400 pounds of elk meat on the back of his pickup. Instead, he was sharing his cab with a large, angry wolf that had for some strange reason, saved his life. He now felt a bond with her that he had only experienced back in the day; in Vietnam with his team – a special forces, 'snatch squad'.

Only four of them from their eight strong team had survived until they'd 'reached the world'. Hunter had been captured by the Viet Cong and had spent three years as a prisoner. His closest friend, 'Mickey' had evaded capture mainly due to his own selflessness and had been released by the army quickly due to mental health issues.

Although Mickey was originally from North Dakota, he had bought a farm in Arizona which was where Hunter was from, with the small funds that the army had given him. Also, this was the only area that he could have afforded due to the country's pittance towards veterans.

Mickey had set up the desert farm living on his own small army pension, waiting for years for Hunter's release. It was their farm; something they could do together. They didn't really know what they would do but it would be something they could make work, because they were a good team.

Two months before Hunter made it back to 'the world', Mickey shot himself in the head using the AK47 that he had smuggled back to America along with other weapons and ammunition.

Hunter had found his body and buried his friend on their farm with great sadness. Mickey had left the deeds to the property along with a note to Hunter which simply said,

"Sorry, best buddy! I can't do this anymore. Please go say hello to Ma sometime; tell her I love her but can't be with her, or 'you'."

Mickey had developed such psychotic tendencies that he would try to kill anyone in his vicinity, every time he awoke from sleeping. For this reason, he kept himself away from his beloved Ma for her own safety and when he heard that Hunter was coming home, it was too much of a risk for him, even Hunter would not have been able to solve his problem.

Hunter stopped the old pickup to open the large wooden gates that guarded the driveway leading up to the house. It was a large detached property, just outside of a town called 'Gackle', one of the first houses to be built in this area in the '30s. Very big and very private. The name of the town, Gackle, always seemed to amuse Hunter, and the first day that he and Mickey met, he asked the usual question, "Where you from?" On hearing Mickey's reply, Hunter burst into laughter and said something about breeding geese up there – "Gackle, gackle, gackle!" Mickey just punched him and the two of them went into a 'tear up' before being pulled apart by the army instructors. Mickey was a lot bigger than Hunter but had been impressed by the little guy's ferociousness.

"We're going to see an old friend, wolf. You be nice to her, OK?"

The wolf just gave him a sideways look. She was in pain and she was annoyed; no amount of licking her wound would fix the problem. Maybe she would have to trust this human.

Hunter drove up the long driveway to the house that he had visited a few days earlier.

"Mickey, is that you?" a little old lady shouted from the porch.

"No, it's me, Ma – Hunter. Mickey is back on the farm. He said he's sorry he couldn't come but he's working hard and sends his love," Hunter repeated the same words that he had said a few days previously.

Ma in her own mind was still waiting for her son to come home and would not countenance anything else.

Hunter and Mickey had met on their first day of basic training after volunteering to join the US Army in 1966, 12 years previously. Both were 18 years old and had the same mindset; Why wait to be drafted? Let's just get in and get it over with. Besides that, they were both 'gun freaks' and superb shots. Even their drill sergeant had been amazed at their accuracy and attitude towards army life.

"You boys remind me of me! You are natural born killers!"

They had arrived for their first tour of duty in Vietnam just in time for the 'Tet' offensive in 1968, and had performed so well in the battle for Saigon that they were selected for special forces training and had both been flown back to America for this intensive course.

The two friends became inseparable, even to the point of taking most of their army leave together. Half the time spent in Arizona with Hunter's sister June, since his own mother and father had died quite young; she was the only direct family member he had left and the other half in North Dakota at the house that Hunter and the wolf had just arrived at.

Ma was like his second mother who treated him as her second son. Hunter hugged her and she was grateful to see him again but suddenly noticed.

"Hunter, you have a strange smell about you. Whatcha been doing, sleeping with dogs?"

"Not exactly Ma, but I do have a friend with me; can I bring her in?"

"Did you say 'her', Hunter?"

Ma asked loudly watching him limp back to the old pickup.

"Sure thing, Hunter, any friend of you and Mickey's is a friend of mine, so what's up? Have you finally found yourself a girlfriend?"

"Well, she's a girl but I can't say she's my friend; she doesn't like me that much," Hunter replied looking back.

Hunter opened the door of his pickup and the wolf looked up to him. The look in her eyes told him she was starting to become sick. He put his hand on her neck which she allowed and felt her temperature rising.

"Come on, girl. Let's get you fixed up."

The wolf got up unsteadily and yelped as she landed on all fours, her wound causing her pain.

Ma looked at the wolf in amazement as she limped toward her.

"Oh, look at the beautiful hairy doggy. Come here, girl...let me see you."

The wolf obeyed the old lady and walked straight toward her, allowing herself to be stroked and caressed, sniffing at her face and ears at the same time.

"I like this human, she smells of 'care'."

"Oh yes, oh yes, we do like you," Ma answered, kissing the wolf's nose and lips, but then looked down to the wound on her shoulder and saw the first signs of festering beginning to appear; this was bad and suddenly Ma got serious herself.

"Hunter, get some blankets from the spare bedroom, you make her comfortable on the porch here while I fix us up a poultice. Do you have any stitching stuff? She is gonna need stitching after we get the poison out."

Hunter knew not to argue with Ma and hurried to make the wolf a comfortable bed. He returned to the pickup, finding an old army-issued first aid kit that had been supplied to his special forces unit, which included butterfly stitches and a couple of morphine hits that he wondered about, if they would work on a wolf?

She just looked at him suspiciously and growled, as he made her up a bed on the porch. She laid on the blankets offered to her still staring at his eyes, trusting the little, old lady but still not him.

Ma was inside the house soaking a large piece of lint in boiling water mixed with herbs that she had gathered from her garden. She let the brew cool down slightly before bringing the steaming bowl outside and sat next to the wolf who was laid on her right side, on the bed made up by Hunter.

Ma held the wolf's head, looked into her big eyes and explained to her.

"Now this is going to hurt just a little bit, doggy so don't you go biting me, OK?"

The wolf acknowledged this with a quick sigh and then closed her eyes awaiting the treatment.

The gentle old lady picked up her healing poultice from the pot and laid it upon the wolf's wound. Her eyes opened sharply at the initial pain and she began to struggle.

"Hold her, Hunter," Ma ordered and he held onto her back quarters until the initial pain subsided and she felt a warm feeling overcome her wound.

"I trust you she-human, tell him to let go of me."

"OK, Hunter, let her go now."

Ma then lightly bandaged the poultice in place and sat back to wait.

"Take about an hour before we have to do the stitching Hunter; are you gonna be ready for that?"

"Do you have any cigarettes in the house, Ma?" Hunter asked. He had not partaken for a couple of days and was now desperate for a smoke. His last pack was now laying, scattered in the snow, back in Canada.

"You know where they are Hunter, but don't take them all; you know what Mickey's like when he runs out of cigarettes. I'd hate to have him come back here and find out you'd smoked them all. We'd both be in big trouble."

Hunter walked into Mickey's bedroom. A few days earlier he had stayed overnight in the guest room and had not wanted to enter this room of homage to his old friend. It had been left the same way as Mickey had always left it. His prized collection of shotguns old and new adorned one wall. The unmade bed and the bedside table which held an ashtray still full of old cigarette butts. A near full pack of Marlborough and Mickey's own Zippo lighter simply engraved with the initials MT – Michael Tomlin sat next to the ashtray. Hunter picked up the photograph behind the bedside lamp and saw Ma between himself and Mickey, both of them smiling like idiots. They had been proudly wearing their new army uniforms, having just completed basic training. They had never been pictured wearing their 'special forces' uniform; that hadn't been allowed.

Mickey had been an only child, his father had died when he was very young, and his whole world revolved around his Ma and hers around him. Hunter had been a welcomed addition to their small family having had a similar upbringing.

Hunter picked up the old pack of Marlborough and took out two cigarettes which he left beside the ashtray along with Mickey's Zippo.

"That's for when you come back, buddy."

Hunter searched in his pockets for his own precious Zippo before he realised that he must have lost it back in the snow. He found some matches in the kitchen and lit up a smoke, coughing due to the age of the tobacco. He walked outside to the porch.

Ma was still cradling the head of the wolf in her hands who looked at Hunter as he breathed smoke into the evening sky.

"Am I with a dragon?"

"You finish that cigarette, Hunter, then go and wash your hands; shame we ain't got nothing to calm her down. This is gonna hurt her."

Hunter then realised that he had spent the last hour in Mickey's room reliving old times.

He washed his hands in the kitchen and then showed Ma the morphine from his kit. A small flexible file with a needle covered with a plastic tube.

"I have this, Ma?"

The old lady quickly looked at the capsule before deciding.

"OK then but not too much. Just try half of that…just squeeze a little bit; if she starts biting me, give her the rest."

Ma held the wolf's head talking to her, reassuring her before finally nodding to Hunter who jabbed the needle into her hind quarters and squeezed the file of drugs. Quickly retracting the needle, he leapt onto the wolf who was struggling to get up. He and Ma couldn't hold her as her head went up and with her last remaining piece of strength, she let out a huge, "*AHOOOOOOOOOOoo!*"

After a short while she calmed and laid back down, the morphine taking affect.

Ma worked quickly taking the butterfly stitches from Hunter, knitting the tough skin together, six in all.

The wolf finally became unconscious as she stitched the last one before covering the operation with another light bandage.

They made her comfortable on the porch as she drifted off into a deep sleep.

"Get me a whiskey, Hunter," Ma ordered and he hurried into the kitchen before coming out with a full bottle of Woodford Reserve bourbon and two glasses. This was Ma's favourite brew.

Ma sat on her rocking chair with Hunter sitting on the steps of the porch sipping whiskey.

"Hey, Hunter, do me a favour would ya?" the old lady asked.

"Sure Ma."

"Take some frozen elk out of the freezer unit. I'm sure your 'wolf' would like some when she wakes up; that's if she does wake up boy – she's in a bad way."

Hunter realised that he had to explain what had happened to him.

"Ma, she is not 'my wolf'; she saved my life, if anything, I'm her human," Hunter answered before reliving the events of the past 36 hours.

"Yea well do that anyway and go have a bath. You smell like a wolf; after that I'll take a look at your feet."

"What's up?" Hunter tried to lie.

"You don't fool me sonny; you've been walking like a flea in a frying pan since you got here. Go wash up and I'll fix you a foot tonic."

"Sure thing, Ma."

"By the way, whatcha call this beautiful hairy lady?"

"I just call her wolf, Ma."

"Well, I wanna call her 'Winter'," Ma announced remembering the story that Hunter had just told her.

"Gee, thanks, Ma," Hunter answered sarcastically.

Ma just laughed a loud, crackly mad-old-lady laugh.

Hunter had his first full bath in a long time in the first-floor bathroom before dressing himself in his only other change of clothing. He hobbled down the stairs barefooted to let Ma inspect his blackened toes.

"Hunter, you are going to lose both your small toes and maybe one big toe. Didn't Mickey tell you about the sudden changes of weather up there?"

"Yes, he did ma'am," Hunter answered respectfully.

Ma shook her head before answering.

"Well, I can't do anything about them. I can just make you comfortable for a while; you'll have to see a doctor or maybe even go to hospital when you get home."

"Sure thing, Ma." Hunter's ability to deal with pain was immense. He had been tortured regularly during his time locked in a filthy prison, and after a while, pain just seemed to go away.

Hunter sat with his feet in a bowl full of Ma's brew for the next couple of hours.

They both carried on sipping whiskey until Hunter fell asleep on the porch near the wolf. He hadn't slept in a bed for 10 years or more. Ma covered them both up with another blanket from the spare room, before sitting back in her rocking chair thinking deeply about what to do next.

***

Hans Schnell was in the lobby of his hotel having just finished an interview with CNN television. He dried his tears with a handkerchief as the crews packed up their equipment. Two Chippewa Indians stood by the hotel bar and Hans beckoned for them to follow him to his room.

All three sat down in the room and Hans went directly into business mode.

Opening up a briefcase, he pulled out a bundle of American dollars and held the cash towards one of the Indians.

"Ten thousand dollars, and there will be another ten thousand when you bring me proof that the wolf is dead."

"What about the guy?"

"I don't care about him at all – do whatever you want. I just need you to kill the wolf."

The two Indians took the cash and headed towards the border crossing – the same one that Hunter had used two days earlier.

Hans hurried to pack. He needed to be back at his office in Geneva as soon as he could. His time as a police detective had been dealing with international money laundering and he had a few friends in the FBI that owed him favours. He had instructed the Chippewa Indians – George Cohen and John Crow to book into a hotel the other side of the border. From there they would make contact with him in Switzerland to receive further instructions. He knew that the information he required would have been hand written into a log of incoming people and vehicles by the border guards, not something anyone could just walk up and demand from them. He would get this information, but it would take time.

This was good. Hunter needed all the time he could get.

***

The next morning the wolf gradually awoke. Ma and Hunter had watched over her throughout the night. Hunter never slept more than two hours at any one time and they both wondered about the effects of morphine on such a creature.

They were both happy with her recuperation and watched her closely over the next two days, sleeping on the porch and occasionally getting up for her functions and a wander around.

Hunter stayed with her all this time. Ma didn't sleep much either and kept a careful watch over both of them.

One day a shout came over the large gates that protected the property from outsiders.

"Mrs Tomlin! Mrs Tomlin are you there?"

Ma and Hunter looked at each other and down to the wolf who was beginning to stir at the sound of a foreign voice.

"Get her inside, Hunter, put her on Mickey's bed; you still smell like a wolf, he might as well be the same," she whispered.

Hunter gently picked up the still-sick creature and placed her on top of his old friend's unmade bed. Her eyes opened for a second and she growled softly. He stroked her head and said,

"Glad to see you alive, wolf."

She sniffed at his odour and recognised him even though he had washed and then closed her eyes to sleep once again.

"Yea I'm here, what do you want?" Ma shouted out to her neighbour that she hadn't had contact with for the past year.

"I just wanted to check that you are OK. Have you seen the news? There is a wolf at large in North Dakota and I thought I heard one howl around here the other night."

"It was probably that darned fox that's been dogging my chickens for the past month. I shot him with a bb gun."

"Oh well as long as you're OK? Take it easy ol' girl and look out for the wolf – she's a killer."

"How do you know that?"

"I seen it on TV. This guy says it killed his wife in Canada and then made it across the border into America."

"Where the hell is Canada?"

"Not far from here, Mrs Tomlin."

"Oh well, don't you worry about me. I can look after myself."

"I know you can, Mrs Tomlin. I just wanted to make sure."

Ma walked into the house and confronted Hunter and the she-wolf in Mickey's bedroom; her still fast asleep.

"What happened?" Ma asked Hunter who had listened carefully to the conversation.

"I don't really know. Have you got a TV Ma? Maybe there's something on the news."

"Yes, I do, Hunter, but you must promise me that you won't do what you normally do with TVs. I have one hidden cause I knew you were coming."

"Awww!" Hunter moaned.

Hunter's passion was television. He could sit and watch TV the whole day long unless a politician appeared on the screen. If one did, then he would grab his nearest weapon and blow the hell out of it. That was Hunter's mental issue; he couldn't help himself. He hated any kind of authority that would make life or death decisions but would never dirty their own hands.

Ma produced a small 14-inch television and plugged in the aerial connection and the power. The black and white screen flashed into life and they found a news channel. Ma poured them a couple of whiskeys and Hunter lit another stale Marlborough coughing slightly as he took his first drag. After a while, the story that they had been waiting for arrived.

"We're now going back to Regina, Canada for the shocking story of a wolf, killing a defenceless woman."

The picture moved to a crying 'Hans Schnell' who was being questioned by a reporter.

"Mr Schnell, we're all sorry to hear about your wife. Please explain how this happened; why were you near the wolves?"

"We were studying them – doing research for the Canadian Forestry Commission. All of us were unarmed when they attacked. I was lucky to get away with my life but my poor Helga…" Hans went into another bout of crying.

"I'm sorry, Mr Schnell. This must be a very difficult time for you but how do we know a wolf is now at large in America?"

"We saw it running. It had blood everywhere – in its mouth and then the beast ran to a truck with a man. He opened the door and then the monster got in. We chased them all the way to the border but of course I am Swiss – I only had the visa for Canada so I could not follow."

"So, Mr Schnell you are saying that a man, possibly American has brought this 'dangerous animal' into our country?"

"Yes…yes, you must all beware! This wolf is a killer – you must find it."

"Thank you, Mr Schnell. Lynsey Looper, CNN."

Ma switched off the TV and quickly hid it having noticed Hunter going into one of his 'rage traces' – the sure sign that he was going to blow the TV apart. She left him until the cigarette he was holding burnt its way down to the tip. Shaking his hand with the small amount of pain he came out of his trance, trying to grasp at whatever weapon was around.

"Hunter, calm down," Ma ordered gently and he did so.

***

"That is one lying coyote son of a bitch, worse than a politician hombre." Hunter replied, now out of his angry trance.

"I do agree with you, Hunter. I could see that even his back teeth were lying. So what do we do now? That is our question," Ma said taking a sip of whiskey.

Just then the two of them turned to see the wolf standing in the doorway, her long toothy mouth open and panting.

Hunter rushed to get her a bowl of fresh water which she lapped up generously while Ma took off her bandage to inspect her wound and fussed over her. Hunter then produced a bowl of raw elk meat which she sniffed at before gently chewing at the meal.

"Thank you, beast."

"I think she's made it through Hunter – festering's gone. I can't see no yellow puss anymore – anyhow will be a couple of days before she's good to go."

"Go where? I want to stay here."

"Well, she sure as hell can't stay here, I can imagine the amount of bounty that's on her head right now and Mickey's truck is gonna lead them, right here."

"I'm gonna take her home with me; Mickey and I can look after her and maybe you could come visit."

"What? Take her to Arizona? Are you kidding me? The heat alone would kill her. No, boy! She needs her own kin; there is a place not too far from here. Do you know where Wisconsin is, Hunter?"

"Yea, it's sort of 400 miles that way," Hunter pointed in the general direction of east.

"There's a place called Chequamegon-Nicolet."

"How do you say that again?"

"Yea well, it's a national forest area that covers over a million and a half acres of forest and I've heard that there are wolves there. Ain't nobody gonna find her there, Hunter – nobody! It's two large areas of forest. Nicolet is the biggest and I've heard of a river that flows through that place – it's called 'Wolf River'. I can't think of a better place where there might be wolves."

"Am I in this conversation, humans? Whatever you are saying, it doesn't make sense to me."

"Makes sense to me, Ma," Hunter replied not really knowing but already planning.

"You gotta be careful, Hunter. Lot of bears live there too – black bears; they can be mighty unfriendly."

Hunter thought that this was a half-good sort of a plan. He just had to get her to this place then 'release her into the wild'.

"Do you have enough gas in your refrigerator wagon, Hunter?"

"Sure do, Ma. Filled it up just before I got here."

"Good boy! Get it out of the barn and don't put the pickup in there; don't even try to hide it. I know they'll be a coming and I want them to find it."

"Are you sure Ma? Are you gonna be OK?"

"Who me? Don't you worry 'bout a thing, Hunter. When they get here, I'm gonna tell them exactly where you've gone and what to expect to find when they get there! So you had better be ready for them boy!"

Hunter smiled as Ma went into hysterical laughter. Maybe they should cut down on the whiskey, or maybe not; this was beginning to feel like old times.

Mickey had thought of everything in regards to shooting elk. He had often told Hunter of his ideas during his visits to Arizona.

"See, Hunter, just kill one of them and you can have free meat for a whole year! As long as you don't mind eating elk every day."

He had purchased a small truck with a refrigeration box on the back that would be driven to Ma's house in North Dakota. He would then take the pickup and hidden weapons to Canada and make the kill. Back at Ma's place, he would butcher the animal, leaving enough in her freezer unit to last for a year. After which, he would transport the rest of the 'free' meat to Arizona in the refrigerated vehicle.

He had not himself been able to put his meatgathering plan into action for Arizona but on his release from the army, a couple of years previously, had visited his beloved Ma and had taken the old pickup across the border to successfully gather meat as he had done in the past, and indeed the elk that still remained in her freezer unit was from this mission.

The fact that Mickey had actually 'killed' something had probably saved his mother's life. His killing need had been sufficed for a while before he took a long train journey back to the farm in Arizona. That had been the last time she saw her loving son.

Hunter returned to the guest bedroom and covered his feet with a brand-new pair of socks. This act was the most wonderful thing in his life and after putting on his boots, that were finally beginning to wear in, he danced a stupid little dance to the quiet sounds of a Marcus Malone song on the radio, *'Double Dee Double Dee – Double Delight'*. He was happy for a short moment.

Hunter moved the vehicles around and retrieved everything of value including his own M16 from underneath Mickey's pickup and put it behind the seats of the refrigeration wagon that he had driven all the way from the farm in Arizona. Mickey had purchased the vehicle directly from a hospital that had wanted to upgrade their stock. In the past, it had been used to carry frozen blood samples from one hospital to another and in the glove compartment was a sign saying, 'Blood Delivery' in bold letters that could be placed on the dashboard. Hunter's mind was working – rummaging around found a small badge that could be pinned to his shirt simply saying, 'Blood Courier'.

"This could work," he said to himself. He then ran his eyes over some maps of North Dakota, Minnesota and Wisconsin, planning his new route. He didn't even bother looking at the way home to Arizona that would come later, if he made it, that was.

Walking back into the house, he noticed the pain in his feet had eased slightly due to Ma's foot tonic. He walked towards the guest room and looked in the open doorway of Mickey's room on the ground floor to see Ma asleep on the bed, snoring gently. The wolf's head laid on her small belly, her left leg reaching over as if in protection. She looked up to him for a second before closing her eyes and continued sleeping along with the gentle little, old lady.

***

Mickey had a wealth of army-issued equipment stored in the basement. Hunter was well aware of this. Every time they had been given leave, they would take what they could home. At first, they had to smuggle the gear away in another one of Mickey's pickup trucks, but when they had both completed their 'special forces course', they just had to show their badge; no other questions were asked.

Hunter entered the room and looked at the racks of M16s alongside some AK47s. He rooted around and began with dusting off an old rucksack. He knew that he would be travelling light and didn't need much on this mission; he just wanted to find 'a few special things'. Hunter did not like hand guns but threw in a Colt45 in its holster along with detachable round clips of ammo, just in case. The handle was an off-white mother of pearl colour that always reminded Hunter of General George S Patton and every time that Mickey had proudly produced this weapon and waved in front of Hunter's face, he would stroke the handle and quietly say, "Arsehole." Hunter had never been a fan of authority.

He then came across something that even he didn't know that Mickey had taken – a claymore mine! The curved metal object was wrapped with sticky tape that had degraded and the arming wire with its loop was hanging ready for action.

"Yea, might as well have that for a 'bit of fun'," he said to himself as he carefully placed the object to one side, wrapped up in Mickey's wet weather cape.

He then filled the rucksack with a month's worth of emergency food rations looking forward to the disgusting taste of Cajun chicken once again.

He threw in 20 clips of 30 round magazines for the M16 and thought for a moment before adding one more 'for good luck'.

"Set to go."

Hunter was in debt to the wolf and he was not going to let her die without a fight. He already knew how to fight when he had joined the army...but then – America trained him.

***

George Cohen and John Crow were in a motel room just south of the border crossing, making a long-distance call to Geneva, Switzerland.

The black ATV with blackened windows was parked outside. It had been 'lent to them' courtesy of Hans Schnell and after a few hours of modification in one of their families' garages, had two secret compartments welded onto the vehicle. One small one held a stash of American dollars behind the glove compartment and the other, weapons, which included an M16 with huge, long Russian sights. The border guards had torn the vehicle apart at the crossing but still missed the cleverly designed subterfuge.

John Crow made the call, pen and paper in hand.

"Hello, Mr Schnell. It was touch and go but we made it."

"Yes, well I have all the information that you need. Please listen carefully."

Hans proceeded to give the Indian trackers the license plate number of the pickup and the address from where it was registered in Gackle, North Dakota.

The vehicle is registered to a Michael Tomlin. My friends have found out that he was in the American army but even they could not find anything else because the information concerning him was classified.

John Crow nodded knowingly, yea – special forces.

"OK well, we'll do our best, Mr Schnell."

"Just kill the wolf, please."

George and John had also survived a tour of Vietnam in the regular infantry and they sort of knew what they were up against. Killing the wolf wouldn't be a problem; they had done that all their lives. The guy however would be different, more challenging, even so they laughed between themselves as they shared a customary cigarette together.

"We gonna hunt White Man!"

***

Hunter made some coffee and the aroma woke Ma from her sleep.

Ma and Hunter sat silently at the kitchen table drinking coffee. The wolf sat on the floor next to Ma who stroked her head which she allowed and enjoyed. In return, she rubbed her face against the little, old lady's tiny leg.

"You ready for the mission, Hunter?" she suddenly asked.

This comment took Hunter right back to the assembly point back in Vietnam. The sound of the helicopters warming up filled his ears.

The air cavalry would get them in, and hopefully get them out again. He loathed these people.

"Hey, special forces, you get in the 'shit' out there; just give us a call, we'll come and get ya!" Yes, he really did hate those people.

"Yea, Ma – good to go."

"Think you might need these," she said standing up and handing Hunter a couple of packs of Marlborough along with Mickey's Zippo that she had refilled with lighter fluid and a bottle of her favourite whiskey – Woodford Reserve.

"Thanks, Ma. I think Mickey wants this back in Arizona," Hunter spoke holding the lighter, turning it around and flicking the top.

The little, old lady got down on her knees and looked straight into the wolf's eyes who began to look worried.

"You have to go now doggy; as much as I love's ya, I can't come with ya. You have to go with Hunter now."

"With him?"

"Yes, girl! He's gonna take you back to you own kin, he's gonna take care of you so don't you worry."

The wolf got up obediently and followed Hunter out of the house and down the steps of the porch. Hunter fired up the refrigeration wagon and moved it forward next to the house, opening the passenger door. The wolf took one more long look at Ma before hobbling around her yard, urinating and leaving scat around the whole area, marking out her territory, before leaping onto the passenger seat of the vehicle, pawing and scratching at the unfamiliar upholstery as she had done before.

Ma ran up to the gates at the end of the driveway and opened them up before quickly closing them again as the wagon left. She then went back into her house and poured herself a large whiskey, planning for the visit from the 'bad guys' that she knew would come.

***

Hunter reckoned that if they were to be stopped and searched then it would be at the state line crossing. The blue flashing lights in the distance confirmed his suspicions.

He pulled off the main road into a quiet industrial park and beckoned the wolf to follow him to the back of the vehicle. Opening up the double doors, he placed a couple of blankets on the floor onto which she leapt, now understanding the need to hide.

As Hunter shut the doors, he put a customary finger to his lips and uttered, "Schuuuuuussssss."

"If you keep saying that awful sound to me, Human, I will bite your hand off."

"Its gonna get cold in here girl but you are a wolf, and you can deal with that, eh?"

"Maybe I should just kill you right now, human? How would you feel about that?"

Hunter locked up the door and as he drove away, turned the temperature control for the refrigeration unit all the way to -30 degrees maximum coldness.

The wagon joined an endless line of vehicles held up by the police road block. He moved the 'Blood' sign to the middle of the dashboard and clipped on his blood courier badge. After one hour, he made it to the check point and a light shined on him and then to his sign in the front window.

"Hello, sir. We are carrying out vehicle checks, where are you heading?"

"Hi, officer. I'm taking frozen blood samples to the University of Minneapolis Hospital."

"Out kinda late, aren't you?"

"The medical profession never stops, sir. I have to get them there by first thing tomorrow morning."

"I still need to take a look in the back if that's OK with you."

"Not really, officer. That could compromise the samples if you opened it up; look at the dial here – its minus thirty back there."

The police officer shone his torch into the cab and took a look at the dial.

"That's actually reading minus 50, sir."

Hunter was shocked momentarily. He had misread the gauge in the dark cabin.

"Well, its dam cold anyhow."

"I guess you're right, sir. Not even a wolf could survive that cold."

The police officer moved the barrier but then came back to Hunter's window.

"Just have to ask, sir – there's a funny smell in your cabin, what is that?"

"I ate some bad Cajun chicken earlier on officer, been farting my arse off ever since."

"Oh man get out of here, go see someone at the hospital when you get there."

"I sure will, sir." Hunter smiled as he drove the wagon over the county line. He turned off the refrigerator unit quickly and drove as fast as he could looking for a quiet area to get the wolf out of the cold room.

He found a lorry park and quickly reversed in between two huge trucks.

He ran to open the back doors not knowing what to expect and a fog of cold air blew into his face.

"You OK wolf?" he asked quietly.

Her big eyes glared at him angrily; small drops of ice hung from the sides of her toothy jaw that was frozen together and she shook uncontrollably.

"I am going to kill you, beast, unless you kill me first."

Hunter quickly got another blanket from the front seats – the ones she had been laying on were frozen stiff – and carried her to the passenger seat, careful not to disturb her wounded shoulder which she could not actually feel at this time. Making her stiff body as comfortable as he could, he quickly shut the rear doors and drove out of the lorry park turning the heat on full.

He drove on for another hour heading east through Minnesota, taking glances down to the wolf who was slowly beginning to thaw. Gradually decreasing the heat in the cab, he noticed her beginning to stretch her legs and eventually, she shook off the blanket that covered her. Hunter breathed a sigh of relief. "Sorry 'bout that, girl. Guess I'll have to go get my eyesight checked soon."

The wolf gave him a split-second, angry look before pawing away at her seat. She pushed the blanket into the foot well and made herself comfortable on the seat before sleeping.

***

George Cohen and John Crow parked their ATV in front of the large wooden gates at Ma's place. John Crow ran around the back of the property and leapt over the six-foot fence before sneaking his way to the barn. Seeing the pickup truck and checking out the number plate, he found it was all he needed to know. George Cohen made the next move. He pushed at the large gate and it opened with a creak from the rusty hinge holding the structure.

"Hey, Mickey, is that you?" a faint voice from the house spoke.

George Cohen walked into the property and looked around suspiciously before slowly walking down the long drive way toward the main house. He could smell wolf and noticed the few scat droppings scattered around the yard.

Ma was sitting in her rocking chair on the porch; a blanket covered her small legs.

George Cohen headed towards Ma, and just as he came into view, she spoke in her old granny voice...

"You ain't my Mickey, where is he?"

"That's what we want to know, lady. We ain't gonna hurt you – we just want to find Mickey."

"We?" she asked quietly looking flustered. "Are there more of you?"

George Cohen beckoned John Crow to come over from the shadow of the barn. He walked towards the house and as soon as he put his first foot on the steps leading up to the porch, Ma pulled back her blanket and stood up to reveal a pump action shotgun with a sawn-off barrel which she quickly loaded with the first shot. It was another one of Mickey's hybrid weapons.

"Don't move boys; if you do then, I will fire this weapon and you should both know that I have eight shots at my disposal."

The Chippewa Indians froze in shock, looking at the old lady and her weapon. They agreed with everything she had said and put their hands up in surrender. She had them both bang to rights in a deadly crossfire – if she pulled the trigger, the shot would hit both of them, they knew this. The Indians had been outwitted by a little, old lady. Ma held her nerve and kept a bead on the Indians as she lowered her small arms to make herself comfortable – the shotgun was heavy.

"What are you two Injuns doing on my property? Any chance you're looking for a wolf?"

"Yes, ma'am, we are."

"Which one of you sons of bitches shot her?"

The two Indians exchanged glances before answering.

"We didn't know she'd been hit, lady."

"Oh yes, she was. I fixed her up – what happened out there?"

John Crow felt a pang of guilt. It had been his job to protect 'Helga', the wife of Hans Schnell, but had been more excited about the slaughter of the pack and had left her alone in the woods, thinking she would be safe.

"It would have been the boss's wife – her weapon had been fired."

Ma nodded knowingly.

"That the woman she killed? What happened to the rest of the pack?"

"They all died, ma'am."

She stood in sadness and respect at the loss of her lovely doggy's family.

"Well, boys, because I 'don't like you, I'm gonna tell you exactly where she has gone."

The Chippewa Indians listened intensely, their hands still raised above their heads.

"Chequamegon-Nicolet."

They looked at each other, very familiar with this area; they even had a lot of family there.

"That's a big place, ma'am – can you be more specific?"

"I'll give ya a little clue, boys. Next to what river would you expect to find wolves?"

"Wolf River? There's actually more bears there than wolves, ma'am."

Ma shrugged her shoulders a little bit in embarrassment; she had guessed wrong.

"Well anyhow, when you get there you are gonna find at least one angry wolf and my son Mickey waiting for ya. He is gonna get ya and she is gonna bite both of your sad arsehole's afore she gets to her own kin and maybe her new family will also chew on your dead bones."

Ma knew that she had said too much.

"Thank you, ma'am. Can we go now?"

Ma thought for a while and ushered the Indians to stand back from the porch.

"Not before you have a drink with me."

Ma picked up a full bottle of whiskey and pulled the cork out with her teeth before spiting it aside. Taking a swig, she threw the bottle to George Cohen who drank a mouthful before handing the bottle to John Crow who followed suite. He then threw the bottle back to Ma and the whiskey went around until the bottle was finished. She dropped the empty bottle down onto her porch, still levelling the heavy weapon towards the Indians studying them for a while.

"So what tribe do you big boys hail from anyhow?"

"We're Chippewa, ma'am."

"Ojibwa eh!" the old lady surprised them by using the ancient term for their tribe.

"Well, I guess I've just sent my son and his wolf right into your back yard, so now, if you don't mind, will you two dammed Injuns – GET OFF MY PROPERTY!"

She fired the first shot into the air as the two Indians ran to the safety of their ATV feeling the next few shots going over their heads. Ma then chased them like a mad banshee, firing shots above their heads and screaming warnings until she reached the gates and watched them depart – looking closely at the back of their vehicle as it sped away.

A little while later she was snoozing on her porch with the shotgun still resting on her lap.

"Mrs Tomlin, are you OK?" the concerned neighbour shouted.

"Yea, what's up?"

"I thought I heard gunshots."

"It was that dammed fox again. I think I got him this time."

"I'm sure you did, ma'am."

***

Hunter's plan was simple – he didn't have a plan, so he just made up a few easy rules. Sleep by day – travel by night – have no contact with anyone unless he had to and that would only be to top up on gas. He would find all-night gas stations for this. Hunter didn't think there was any way on this earth that the wolf would agree to being hidden in the refrigeration unit again, although he'd noticed her perking up after she'd thawed out. Her wound had begun to heal nicely; he could tell this as she occasionally tried to scratch at it with her right paw. "Itching wound is a healing wound, wolf," he advised her once with only a vicious look in response.

Every time he spoke to her, she glared at him for a few seconds before fussing around on the passenger seat. Therefore, he decided to keep conversation to a minimum.

"Be quiet, beast. Your world is confusing me enough without hearing your senseless words."

Hunter had studied the maps taken from Mickey's pickup, looking for quiet areas that they could possibly hide away on their journey. He had calculated, an 18-hour drive would get them to the Chequamegon-Nicolet.

After some thought, Hunter decided that it would be too much in one go for his companion who was still recuperating, and so, he had picked out a place that they might rest for a while – Detroit Lakes Minnesota. It was on the way.

***

George Cohen and John Crow had stopped at a gas station just across the state line near Fargo. George Cohen was making a collect call from the phone booth to Switzerland.

Hans Schnell answered the operator quickly,

"Yes of course, I will accept the charges, put him through."

"Hello, Mr Schnell. We found the truck and we know where he is heading."

"That is good work – good work and do you know the vehicle he is travelling in now?"

"No sir, we don't have that information."

"It is good that I know then – my contacts have given me much more information. They will possibly be in a refrigeration truck that is also registered to Michael Tomlin, but in Arizona. There is one more thing that is strange however; this man does not exist anymore – he committed suicide one year ago; the man you are chasing is not Michael Tomlin."

Although Hunter had shown his passport, the old border guard had not bothered logging down his name or personal details.

"Does this change anything, sir?"

"Not at all – just kill the wolf and him, if you have to, whoever he is."

Hans hung up the telephone and turned the Zippo lighter around in his hand. The initials H.W. burnt into his skin and the place – Arizona revealed another clue. They weren't relevant at this time but he mulled them over all the same.

***

Hunter made a stop in a gas station in the early morning just before he got to Detroit Lakes. He covered up the wolf in a blanket once again just before he ordered the young petrol attendant to fill her up. Just her head was visible and she complied with his request once again. He ran to the phone booth and called Ma who answered immediately.

"How's it going, Hunter?"

"Yea good, Ma. Have they been?"

"Sure have, boy! Two big, dammed Chippewa Injuns. I told them where you were heading like you told me to."

Hunter had not told her to say that but went along with it anyway.

"Good, Ma! What were they driving?"

"They was in a great big, brand-new ATV painted black with blacked out windows and some strange marking on the back, like a flag, all red with a white cross on it. Are they in some sort of medical profession?"

"No, Ma! That's the flag of Switzerland – that's all I need to know."

"How's my girl?"

"She's good, Ma! Gotta go now, love you, Bi."

Hunter hung up the phone quickly; he didn't want to get dragged into a conversation that could have gone on for hours.

He hurried back to his wagon to see the petrol pump attendant shaking in fear, still squeezing the trigger of the fuel pump, gas leaking all over the forecourt.

"That's enough guy, you can stop now," hunter ordered seeing the wolf staring at the young man through the passenger window... She had never seen a black person before and was fascinated by the creature.

"That's a wolf, ain't it?" the attendant asked nervously.

"No man, that's a dog that looks like a wolf; we call her a 'Queen Dog Wolf'. I think she likes you and just wants to say hello. I promise you, she will not hurt you."

Hunter eased open the passenger door and the wolf's toothy snout came out.

"Just put your clean hand there man, and let her sniff you; that's all she wants."

The young man put his left hand toward the wolf's mouth who sniffed and then licked at the fingers before laying back on the seat.

"A different type of human, how strange!"

"See, she likes you dude; you can go on to greater things from here – you have her 'royal approval'. What's your name?"

"Martin," the young man spoke in a state of shock taking thirty dollars from Hunter, ten dollars more than it should have been.

"Catch you later, Martin," Hunter said before quickly driving away from the gas station, rule number two now broken.

They drove on into Detroit Lakes. Hunter wanted to find a secluded area where he could sleep. He didn't have to but he thought it would be wise and would also give the wolf a break from the monotonous journey in the cab. They were out of season for tourists, late autumn and when he had driven for a full hour without seeing any signs of life, stopped near one of the smaller lakes with a wooded area all around them.

Hunter picked up his small binoculars. "Stay here, girl. I'm gonna look around first." She just stared at him.

"Why bother, beast – just ask me!"

Satisfied, Hunter opened the passenger door and she leapt out, her now healing wound not bothering her so much.

Hunter then gathered up some old pine branches and laid them down in a fashion to make himself a comfortable bed. There he slept solid for the next two hours.

"Nice doggy, you are a nice doggy," a little girl's voice spoke.

"I like you doggy – you are coming home with me."

"CHARLOTTE, GET AWAY FROM THAT WOLF!" a man's voice shouted.

"No Daddy! Don't shoot the doggy!"

The man raised his shotgun as the little girl ran away and Hunter screamed in silence as he launched himself between the man with the gun and his wolf.

He felt the shot gently hitting him in the chest and stomach but then awoke suddenly, feeling the wolf pawing at him, holding a large rabbit in her mouth.

It had been a bad dream.

Hunter came to his senses and saw what she had done.

"Oh, man we have dinner!"

She dropped the dead animal to the ground almost as an offering, but then again it might have been a challenge. A culinary challenge.

"You see, wolf, my problem here is, you want to eat this thing raw, but I would like to light a fire – which you probably won't like and cook some of it. Ten years ago, I would have torn this thing apart and ate it just like you, but hey this is 1978 – we're a bit more civilised now, ain't we?"

The wolf just sat aloof and pawed at the dead rabbit as if to say 'go on then'.

Hunter then went back to his wagon and produced a huge hunting knife.

"OK, girl. This might shock you, but I am gonna show you the secret of man's red fire; are you OK with that?"

"Oh, do as you please!"

Hunter gathered up some dry tinder and larger pieces of wood. From the back end of the knife, he pulled out a long piece of iron and as he stroked the sharp steel blade on this item, large sparks appeared and ignited the tinder. He could have used Mickey's Zippo but wanted to make sure some of his old skills remained. Hunter blew at the base before a flame ignited and started to burn the small pieces of wood.

The wolf just sat back and observed, undisturbed by the flames and smoke.

"Not in my world."

Hunter then took out the heart and liver of the small animal and handed them to the wolf who devoured them in one mouthful. The guts and everything that humans would normally throw away were eaten from the palm of his hand. Nothing went to waste in the wolf's world. He then skinned the rabbit and chopped the small animal in half with the large knife offering either side to the wolf, mainly the front half first. She reached over and chose the back section – clever girl!

Hunter put a thin stick through the rest of the small animal and fixed it above the flames of the small camp fire, the meat sizzling nicely, as the wolf ripped into her half of the meal.

"Fire, food, nice surroundings, friendly company – how bout' that wolf? I feel like we're on vacation."

She relaxed herself and lay down on the bed that Hunter had created still staring at him.

"I like to see you happy, human."

Hunter sipped at some whiskey from a bottle that Ma had gifted him and tore little pieces of cooked rabbit from the small dinner. He offered her a small piece but she backed off with a look of disgust.

"You've tried to freeze me, now you're trying to poison me?"

Hunter ate every piece of the meal, even chewing at the bones as the wolf looked on in approval. She had fed 'her human' and felt pleased.

Hunter lit up a Marlborough and quietly began singing a Marcus Malone song.

"Well, I heard it through the grapevine, your big bad wolf is coming home.

"And your little red riding hood is gonna know that you been up to no good.

"But these, comp – comp – complications, are killing me."

Her ears pricked up and turned as he hummed this small tune even though he sang it badly.

Hunter did think about changing the plan and heading straight for Arizona for a split second but then that would leave Ma in a compromised position. No, he would deal with the problem.

Wandering off into the forested area as the wolf relaxed in front of the fire, he picked up a length of old wood about a yard long, sat back down with it next to the wolf and began to whittle with the large hunting knife.

"Hey, girl! Show me your paw."

She looked at him confused for a moment but then he lifted one leg and pointed to the bottom of his boot.

She then lifted her own back leg which she let him hold and study for a while and after a lot more whittling, cleared a small area of pine cones to reveal bare earth, pressed the end of the stick into the soil to reveal a perfect print of a wolf's paw.

"The only way to fight Indians, girl, is to think like one."

Hunter spoke remembering his growing up time back in Arizona where most of his young friends were Apache.

"I'm sure you are correct human, whatever you are saying."

They stayed where they were until the sun began to go down, each enjoying the moment together.

Then it was time to go, the wolf sensed this and ran around squirting urine, marking out the area. She liked this place and had enjoyed the relaxed time with 'her beast'.

Hunter sorted out his equipment carefully emptying the rucksack; he gently placed the claymore mine to one side and fixed it to a shelf in the refrigeration unit of his truck. He didn't want any unstable ordinance rolling around. For this mission, he was lightly armed by his old standards. A beaten up old M16 with twenty-one clips, a large hunting knife and a Colt45 – damned cowboy weapon, he called it.

Mickey's old waterproof hat which would fit him perfectly and a wet weather cape that was a few sizes too big. Because the weather in Vietnam and indeed Arizona was so hot, he had never needed any thermo clothes, but after his recent expedition he had raided Mickey's bedroom and found some long johns and a thermo vest; these he put on underneath his clothes, although too big a size – they fitted comfortably and gave him an incredible warm feeling.

Hunter drove through the night still evolving a plan – still making changes; he didn't enjoy that fact that he was being 'hunted' – in the past he had always been the 'hunter'.

They were at a massive disadvantage; the area was huge and he could not hope to find the black ATV with the Swiss flag by just driving around so he would have to leave some bait for them to find. According to the old map of Wisconsin that he had, the edge of the National Park was about 20 miles long – over a hundred camping sites bordered the massive forest. They would be a needle in a haystack. Heading for Wolf River would narrow things down a bit.

Hunter had let the Indians get ahead of him with his stop at Detroit Lakes so now it was a case of 'cat and mouse'. Who is gonna find who first?

Hunter drove into the county of Langdale surrounded by the beautiful forests of the Nicolet. He reckoned that he and the wolf could just jump out of the wagon and disappear at any moment in time, into the lush forest and never be seen again, but that was not what he wanted – Hunter wanted closure one way or the other. He was heading for a town called Lily which was close to Wolf River; he didn't want to go all the way in but on the outskirts, he found what he was looking for – a trailer park.

This would be where the not-so-well-off people lived. Hunter approached the entrance and noticed the office on his left as he stopped. Taking a large swig of whiskey, he put his hand to his mouth and uttered his usual, "Schhhuuuus," towards the wolf.

"Will you stop saying that awful sound?!"

Hunter staggered into the office – it was easy to pretend due to his bad feet.

A Native American Indian sat uninterested behind the counter.

"Hey, dude! Ah need to find somewhere to park up for a few days – do you have any vacant lots? I got some money," Hunter said pulling a few dollars out of his pocket.

The Indian took one look at Hunter and then at the refrigerator wagon that he could just make out through the rain covered window.

"Four dollars a day in advance – no loud parties – don't get drunk and wander around. You can use the wash facilities in the middle of the camp, that's if you want to."

The Indian said sniffing at Hunter's strange odour – wolf mixed with whiskey on his breath…

Hunter picked out a roll of a hundred dollars from his back pocket and handed $30 to the Indian. "I have more."

The Indian shrugged and gave Hunter a pass, "Lot 103, just down there on your left – leave your keys here if you want to leave the compound."

"Thank you, sir," Hunter answered, not giving anything else away and staggered back out of the cabin office.

As Hunter drove the wagon to his allotted space, the Indian picked up the telephone.

"I think your man is here," he said simply.

Hunter reversed the wagon into the allotted space before putting the whiskey and cigarettes away. He never drank or smoked whilst on a mission.

He had set the bait.

Now it all begins. Just at that moment the heavens opened and it began to rain heavily. Hunter put on his rucksack and covered himself in Mickey's cape that came down to around his ankles; he had reluctantly put on the cowboy weapon and knotted the leather holster around his thigh. His well-worn M16 had the customary condom held on with an elastic band over the muzzle. His hunting knife snuggled into the small of his back.

He began to shut and lock the wagon. As he opened the passenger door, he put his hand to one side of the wolf's face which she allowed and said,

"Come on, girl – let's go find your new kin."

"New! I thought that was you! Your world confuses me more and more; why don't we just find a nice place and stay there."

She leapt into the rain and sniffed around while Hunter locked her door.

"This way, girl."

Hunter walked brazenly through the trailer park with the wolf at his side. They reached the office in the pouring rain and he steeled himself. He knew that when he crossed the road there was no going back. Taking a deep breath in, he indicated to the wolf to stay where she was and walked back a few steps to the office door, opening it up just enough to throw the keys toward the Indian behind the reception desk.

At the entrance to the trailer park, they crossed the road and then entered the lush forest to begin heading due north.

The Indian made another call.

"It's definitely him; he's just walked out of here alongside the biggest wolf I've ever seen…oh yea, he was carrying a gun."

Hunter picked up a rough path almost immediately. It was 4 am according to his small, special forces-issued watch and he doubted very much that anyone would be around at this time and in this weather. From the old map he had taken from Mickey's pickup truck, he had worked out a target area. The north lakes of the Nicolet, maybe 40 miles away or more, like 50, the way he was going to travel. If he stayed in touch with Wolf River, this would lead him all the way up; the only other tool he had was a tiny army compass.

He and the wolf strode on; he felt no pain from his feet – he was 'back in the zone'. His main concern was for the welfare of the wolf. This part of his plan left them the most vulnerable so they needed to cover as much ground as possible within the next ten hours. He would only stop if she needed to.

***

As soon as it was first light, George Cohen and John Crow arrived at the trailer park in the black ATV, followed by another truck which held six family members who had been hired up for the hunt. They and the trailer park manager, also a cousin walked down to Hunter's refrigerator wagon and looked around. One of them tried to open one of the back doors but was quickly stopped by John Crow. "Don't touch it!"

Hunter had left nothing of use to them in the cab but they were wise enough not to look in the back.

The Indians parked the ATV right next to Hunter's wagon and began unloading their equipment. George Cohen spoke to four of his cousins to arrange a future meeting point; they were to paddle canoes up Wolf River and rendezvous with the trackers at a point, ten miles upstream.

If they happened to get in front of the quarry and spotted them, they were ordered to shoot to kill – no questions – man with a wolf – shoot both of them.

George Cohen and John Crow led their other two men into the forest and straight away picked up man and wolf tracks in the mud, easily because of the recent rain. The chase was on.

***

Hunter strode on with a purpose, every now and then checking on the wolf. Physically she seemed fine, her tongue hung out of her long toothy open snout which gave her a happy look and it had finally stopped raining. Every so often she would stop and sniff at the air searching for danger. Hunter all of a sudden realised what an asset he had in her.

"I wish I had you with me back in Nam, girl," he thought silently.

"Well, you have me with you now, beast."

Eventually they heard the sound of running water nearby. Hunter guessed correctly that this must be Wolf River. They proceeded with caution until reaching the river's edge. Hunter and the wolf gave each other the split-second look they had developed between each other before she took a long drink and Hunter filled up a water bottle, both of them looking for danger as they did. Hunter then made a move.

The track they were on now ran alongside the river and because of the recent rain their tracks would be obvious to even the most amateur tracker. They turned due west and walked into the thick forest, Hunter taking time to remove all their tracks for the next four hundred yards or so before heading directly north once again; this was easy as the forest was covered in a carpet of old pine needles. Every so often when he noticed clear ground, he would lay down false tracks using the crafted 'wolf paw' stick.

As they headed through thick woods, the wolf felt a bit more at ease.

She hadn't liked the human trail, with the human smell – she was more at home now. Hunter also felt this – he knew whoever was following would eventually rediscover their tracks but would have to hard work for it. Hunter's theory was based around stamina; he would travel all day and all night if necessary, they would be tracking, and that would considerably slow down their progress. He just wanted to complete at least ten miles on this first day which would take them into the dark hours of the next day and maybe get a bit more ahead of them than they would expect. That twinge between his buttocks told him that he was being followed – it would not go away and that annoyed the hell out of him.

***

George Cohen and John Crow easily followed the man and wolf tracks for five miles or so. Their two young cousins began to grow in confidence and one even mentioned the term 'turkey shoot' before the two experienced trackers told them in no uncertain terms to 'be quiet'. They reached the point where Hunter and the wolf had taken a drink, where upon the tracks simply ran out.

The two keen boys ran further up the track and found nothing before running back to the two expert trackers who were both pointing due west. They sent the two young men along the path that followed the river to meet up with their other cousins, another five miles up the rivers course. They didn't need the hindrance of these youngsters knowing that they now had some serious tracking to do.

***

Hunter and the wolf ploughed on through the forest – speed was essential; the more klicks they went, the safer they felt. The rain began again with a vengeance – it poured heavily and Hunter stopped for a while taking cover under a massive tree. He sat with his back against the trunk and opened up half of his wet weather cape to let the wolf share his shelter. She instantly snuggled up to him and he wrapped the oversized canvas around themselves; this was now a familiar feeling between them and they both closed their eyes for a short twenty-minute sleep. The heavy rain stopped as soon as it had started and they both got up as one, heading due north. They must have gone on for another five miles through the forest, before they came upon another man-made path. A well-worn route used by bear hunters. In every memorable waypoint that they stopped at, Hunter hid a couple of M16 magazines already thinking ahead. He remembered the abuse that he used to render towards his old partner back in the day.

"See your problem, Mickey, is that you cannot think anytime past your next coffee break."

"Get out of here, Geronimo!" was always Mickey's response.

This was the personal nickname Mickey had gifted Hunter after one long hot operation. They had made it back to base and Hunter had taken an ice-cold shower, after which his normally pale white skin had turned a deep red colour.

Mickey had noticed this and knowing Hunter was from Arizona announced,

"Hey, guys – we have a redskin in the camp. I bet he's related to Geronimo! Ain't he just as ugly?"

This comment as always ended up in another 'tear up' between the two of them.

Hunter had grown up in Apache country with stories of this amazing man who had evaded capture from the authorities many times. He was pretty much Hunter's growing up hero and as Geronimo was, Hunter always thought in advance. He checked his compass – they were still heading north but this was now miles away from Wolf River. Hunter had noticed how the river had bent around to the east at one point and his change of direction had been made due to this. They would continue on and eventually meet up with the river in a few more miles time. Hunter didn't know the area, he just had a few ideas about where he might go. They walked up the path together; she had not sensed any danger and he now trusted her completely. It headed north and that was all important to him until he came across the sign.

DANGER!
BEAR HUNTING SEASON!

DO NOT TOUCH THE BEAR BAITS!

They carried on regardless. Hunter knew that they would regain touch with the river if they headed directly north. It would naturally curve back around towards them. Another five miles or so he thought, then he would try to get eyes on whoever was following him. The old ordinance survey map he was using showed a bit of rising ground at the point he had chosen. Good ambush country. Every so often he would hear gunshots in the far distance; must be bear hunters, he thought – they'll stay well clear of those people.

***

George Cohen and John Crow caught up with their two young cousins on the trail that followed Wolf River. They had stopped their tracking mission. It was late autumn and a carpet of pine needles covered the forest floor. They soon realised what he had done with his 'wolf paw stick' and had aborted.

They had the skill to track Hunter and the wolf but it would take far too long. Their experience also told them how quickly the unlikely couple were moving. The Indians' only hope was to try to get ahead of them before they disappeared completely. They had a lot at stake, another $10,000 worth of motivation.

Five miles further up the river path, they met up with the other four members of their team – two canoes were tied up to a small wooden jetty.

This was a place where river met lake. 'Pine Lake' in this instance.

The countryside around them was now pretty open but they felt no danger as all stood together discussing their next move.

"They are heading north, and I mean directly north. I don't know how they're doing it but they are travelling very fast."

George Cohen explained.

"Yea that's wolf country, maybe 'Dam Lake', probably 20 – 30 miles from here. I've heard of a wolf pack there," one of the local Indian cousins advised.

"So where do we go from here?" another said to a thoughtful John Crow.

Hunter answered that question.

There was a 'zing' sound of a bullet travelling through the air and then a 'twack' noise as it hit one of the young cousins in the back of his thigh, blood and flesh exploding into the air as the 7.62 mm round passed straight through before they all heard the sound of a shot in the distance.

He fell to the ground and only began screaming when he realised what had happened. John Crow ran to him and began stemming the flow of blood from his upper leg. It was superficial, two inches left and the bullet would have hit his main artery, in which case it would have been 'game over' within two minutes. The rest of the Indians took cover trying to work out the angle that the shot had come from.

A short burst of automatic fire then obliterated the back end of one of the canoes and the small boat began taking on water. John Crow quickly tied up his young cousin's leg with whatever he could find; they hadn't even thought about bringing along a first aid kit.

George Cohen slipped the safety catch on Mickey's M16A1 and surveyed the area where the shots had come from through the huge telescopic sights. Clear as day, he saw a small skinny guy climbing out of a tree and had him bang to rights in the cross hairs. He let off two shots before the figure disappeared into the forest.

They waited a full five minutes listening to the screams of their family member before George Cohen stood up. "It's OK, he's gone."

"He needs a doctor!" one of the other guys shouted.

"Yep, I know he does, and so does he," George Cohen observed.

They quickly put their wounded cousin into the other canoe and two of them began rowing him swiftly down river towards medical help.

Later that evening, after the remaining five Indians had forced marched another few miles north alongside the river path, they lit a fire – drank some whiskey and put on war paint. Up until this point it had been about money, now it was personal. George Cohen beat some sticks against a hollow fallen tree trunk while the rest danced a war dance and chanted a war chant. For three of them, this was the first time they had done this in earnest. George Cohen and John Crow shared a cigarette together in the way they had done in Vietnam before battle.

***

Hunter had climbed down from an old sycamore tree and redressed himself with the rucksack and cape. The unworried wolf was still laid on all fours observing proceedings and glad of the hour rest they had enjoyed. The loud gunshots from Hunter in the tree had made her jump initially but then she saw who was on the end of the weapon.

"Hey, girl. I just drew first blood."

The wolf just glared at him angrily before looking down to her now healing shoulder and back to him again.

"Oh man yea! I'm sorry, girl. They drew first blood! We're gonna have second, third and fourth, before this ends."

"Whatever you say, human – if that's important to you."

Hunter had been in the tree for an hour. It was a precious hour that he had gambled on – it was an 'if' question – if they do this then this will happen – if they do this then that will happen. If they do something else then my arse is screwed…

On the higher ground, he had eventually found a vantage point that looked down to the river 600 yards away. This was the maximum accurate range for a standard M16A1 without telescopic sights; even with them it wasn't much better. He had climbed the old sycamore tree with just the gun and small binoculars and spotted the jetty where two canoes were tied up and four Native American Indians waited… He watched them smoking cigarettes and joking with each other obviously waiting for something or someone to arrive. When they eventually arrived, he knew it was them. One of them carried an M16A1 with huge long telescopic sights. Mickey's gun.

Hunter reckoned that he could have killed at least four of them but this was America, and that would take some explaining to a Judge. Mickey would have killed them all.

This was a back-off call and as he had climbed down from the tree, he felt the 'fizz' of two bullets 'zing' above his head. They must be using Mickey's gun he thought, that damn thing shoots high.

Mickey had painstakingly cut off the carrying handle of his standard issued M16A1 to fit this magnificent set of Russian telescopic sights that he had picked up from a dead Viet Cong sniper that they had routed out on one mission. Try as he might however, he couldn't seem to match the sights with this weapon having made the slightest of errors attaching them with quick release butterfly nuts, and mainly used them for observation purposes.

If he wanted to kill something, he would have to 'shoot low'. Hunter guessed that whoever was shooting at him would have worked this out, so he would not again expose himself as he had done.

***

Hunter and the wolf made speed as quickly as they could, away from the area and as night fell again, they kept on going, needing to be far away before the next sun arose. At 4 am Hunter stopped for a rest; even he was starting to feel the pain. They had travelled another five miles due north up the bear hunters trail, stopping and hiding when either one of them sensed danger; they were becoming a good team, Hunter thought to himself.

He shared two of the emergency ration packs with the wolf, still putting the Cajun chicken to the bottom of the rucksack. They shared water from Hunter's bottle and huddled together underneath Mickey's oversized cape to sleep for one hour.

Hunter and the wolf both woke at the same time after exactly one hour of rest. The rain had stopped and Hunter once again experienced the sudden drop in temperature as the drops of rain were replaced by heavy flecks of snow. He took a quick glance at the wolf who appeared to be smiling at him.

"I can see why Ma called you Winter."

"Welcome to my world, human."

***

George Cohen and John Crow had also sensed the change in weather. Now they were confident of catching their prey. Tracking in the snow was their absolute skill as long as they could stay close enough behind the man and wolf – it would be easy. This was their territory and they were on the war path.

They would overtake Hunter and the wolf undoubtedly, cutting them off at the pass. The Ojibwa were hunting white man and wolf. They would find them, then they would kill them.

George Cohen and John Crow along with their remaining young cousins and now more reinforcements would follow them up to the ambush area somewhere in the North Lakes, somewhere only they knew that a pack of wolves had been spotted in recent months. With Ma's information, they had guessed at Hunter's plan and had even laughed at it. She was a northern grey wolf and even if they got so far as meeting another pack, she would be ripped to pieces by the timber wolves – a different breed entirely.

***

Hunter and the wolf ploughed on regardless, heading directly north through the now settling snow. He guessed that the Indians would camp for the night, so he did the unexpected thing – he kept on going. All through the night he pushed and pushed, stopping for small breaks along the way. The wolf sensed his urgency and kept up with him, not showing any sign of weakness, their mutual bond increasing by the hour. Just before dawn, they stopped for another short break and in the distance they both heard the call of another wolf, "*Ahooooooo*." Hunter looked towards her for a reaction but she remained impassive – maybe she didn't like what she heard, Hunter thought to himself. They made haste through a few inches of snow, in and out of large pine trees. Suddenly, she stopped and sniffed the air. Hunter hadn't seen this in her up until now and was more than concerned as she took off at a run. He followed her tracks and eventually caught up to find her trying to jump up to a huge piece of raw meat that had been suspended in a tree just about out of her reach. 'BEAR BAIT'.

Hunter tried to warn her whispering, "Wolf, wolf," but that had no effect.

Then he remembered Ma's name for her, "Winter! Winter!" To his immense surprise, she stopped jumping for the raw meat and looked towards him as he was hiding behind a nearby tree, beckoning furiously for her to come away from the bait.

In curiosity, she walked towards him and he broke cover to walk towards her.

They both heard it at the same time – it was like a horse galloping.

A massive wolf hound dog ran towards them.

Hunter ran towards the creature shoulder charging it as it leapt in the air. Hunter was knocked senseless by the impact – the thing probably weighed more than he did.

The massive dog recovered quickly and headed towards Hunter, teeth stripped to exact some revenge for his audacity but the wolf grabbed one of its hind legs and hung on, only to be swung aside by the huge dog.

She yelped as it threw her onto her bad shoulder. Hunter reached down for his cowboy weapon but was restricted by his oversized cape. Just as the dog with its mad red eyes was about to wreak vengeance on Hunter, a wolf jumped on to the dogs back and sunk its jaws into the back of its neck.

"That ain't my girl," Hunter thought in a split second as another wolf and then another ripped into the dog. A whole pack of angry wolves then sunk their jaws into the beast. It tried to fight for its life but they held it down until the largest of the pack by far clamped its jaws around the creature's neck, until eventually it stopped moving.

This one then turned its attention to Hunter who was still prone on the ground. It sniffed at the man as the rest of the pack backed off until Winter arrived at his side, growling like a mad banshee, warning the other wolf to leave the man alone. He had sniffed around Hunter and thought that he must be related to her.

Hunter wasn't frightened – he was fascinated! The pack leader and Winter screamed at each other in a tense standoff.

She was much bigger than him but eventually she succumbed to his threats. She had to.

Winter went down on all fours in a submissive fashion and stopped growling. The leader carried on his interrogation close to her head but then became satisfied with the situation. Hunter remained laying on his back in complete silence. Then all was calm. The leader sniffed at Winter, now in a kind way looking down at Hunter, staring at him in the way she had done many times in the recent past.

Then he was gone, the pack followed and Hunter sat upright looking at Winter who stared him in the eyes.

"Thank you, human – I won't forget you."

And then she was gone.

***

Hunter struggled to get up from the snow, his head still dazed from the collision with the monster dog. The sharp pain in his shoulder told him that it was dislocated and he staggered to a nearby tree to push the bone back into place. Hearing a satisfying 'click' he turned to pick up his M16 that he had dropped in the skirmish.

"Don't touch that," a voice ordered.

Hunter looked up to see an Indian pointing a hunting rifle at him – he guessed it was loaded.

"I can't believe you snuck up on me," Hunter said trying to make light conversation.

"I'm an Indian – that's what we do," the man said dryly.

Four more men appeared also carrying hunting guns – bear hunters.

"Jesus Christ, what happened here?" one of them asked looking at the remains of the wolf hound that had been ripped to pieces.

"Wolves killed my dog," the Indian replied angrily before putting his thumb and a finger into his mouth and blowing an almost silent whistle.

Within moments a second massive wolf hound arrived. The huge beast franticly sniffed around the remains of its obvious relative, winning while it pawed at the body. It then put its huge snout in the air and smelled wolf.

Heading straight for Hunter growling as it did, was only stopped from a sharp order from the Indian, "JET! stay boy." The dog stopped short of Hunter. "Guard," the Indian ordered his animal. The beast then snarled loudly at Hunter in a warning mode – if he moved then the highly trained dog would attack.

The Indian was so confident of this that he lowered his weapon and slung it over his shoulder. Although his two dogs were actually wolf hounds, they were mainly used for hunting bear. The four bear hunters had hired the Indian and his dogs for a shoot.

He had raised and trained the two brothers from puppies, now he had lost one and was more than a bit angry about that.

"I've heard about you, mister – you're up here with a wolf, ain't ya?"

Hunter remained silent and went back to the same place that he had been five years earlier in his life when he had been captured by the Viet Cong.

'Say nothing', 'do nothing', 'be nothing.'

"Is that the wolf who killed the woman in Canada and some American guy brought it across the border? I saw that on the news. Is this him?" one of the bear hunters spoke.

"I guess so," the Indian said softly.

"Well, we'd better do something. Shall we tie him up?" another suggested.

"Yea, we can do that," the Indian replied as the men hunted around in their kit to find something to bind Hunter's hands.

The Indian indicated to Hunter to take off his cape and rucksack. As he did so, he spotted Hunter's Colt45 and immediately raised his gun again.

Hunter had thought momentarily about a 'quick draw McGraw' moment with his cowboy weapon but his shoulder was still weak from the dislocation and he couldn't have trusted his right hand. Also, he would have had to kill the Indian, the dog and maybe some of the bear hunters who each carried a hunting rifle. This was 1978 America, he couldn't do that. Mickey would have done, Hunter thought to himself.

Three of the bear hunters picked up Hunter's cape, rucksack and M16 while the other bound his hands behind his back with a lanyard that he had found in their kit. The Indian picked the Colt45 from his holster and also the hunting knife from the small of his back.

"Lead on guys – we have to go meet some friends of mine," the Indian ordered.

***

The snow returned as Hunter was led back down the forest path by the Indian, the excited bear hunters and the huge dog. They stopped at a point that only the Indian knew. He took charge of Hunter's rucksack and M16 before saying goodbye to the bear hunters.

"Just carry on down this track guys – you're camp's about two miles away, you should find it easy enough," the Indian advised.

"What's gonna happen to him?" one of the bear hunters asked.

"Oh, he'll be fine, don't worry about that."

"What about his cape and this old hat, looks like something from Vietnam?"

"Lose it," the Indian ordered.

"Can I keep it?"

"Sure, do what you want."

"Can we have his gun too? That looks like a real M16?"

"Why not?" the Indian answered before handing the old weapon to his clients, confident that Hunter would never ever use it again.

With that, they parted ways.

***

Hunter had never liked John Wayne movies – they were all 'too clean', his clothes were always too clean, the script was always too clean, he always killed all the Indians and got loads of medals.

Hunter didn't even have a 'Purple Heart' – wounded-in-action medal. Mickey had got one but had flushed it down the toilet in a fit of rage one night in Arizona. Their last mission had gone wrong. They had been ambushed at their extraction point. Two of their eight-man team had been killed and he had suffered a small glancing wound to his left shoulder as he had run towards the rescue helicopters.

Hunter had put himself forward as the rear guard, protecting his team as they left their position.

Fire came from the jungle before Hunter attacked them on his own, allowing his team to escape. He had charged and killed 15 Viet Cong soldiers before he realised that the rescue helicopters had all gone.

In the quiet lull afterwards, he had dragged the dead bodies of his 'enemy' into a respectful position side by side in the same open ground and then sat silently with them, hands on head awaiting capture.

'Say nothing', 'do nothing', 'be nothing'.

That had been the world according to Hunter and he was there again.

The Indian and his dog had led Hunter a mile due west through the forest and finally met up with more of his clan. They had a fire going as they walked in. Hunter then thought of John Wayne as he had walked through the Indian camp with the whole tribe staring at him.

"Is that him?" one of the Indians asked. Hunter was just a small skinny little guy with the attempt of a beard on his round face and long wispy grey hair – too grey for his age.

Hunter was made to kneel with his hands bound behind him and slowly looked at the people around him, remembering every face. There were 13 of them Hunter counted, until later on four more entered their camp. George Cohen, John Crow and two young cousins walked in, their bodies covered in a frightening black and white war paint and their faces coloured bright red as if covered with their enemy's blood...

George Cohen and John Crow stood in front of Hunter and stared at the little man. "Hey, he's only a little skinny guy," one of the young cousins shouted. They both ignored this comment; they knew the man in front of them had killed many times before and would do so again given the chance.

"You must be HW – we found your Zippo back there in the snow," George Cohen said referring to the time in Canada.

"All we want is the wolf, the one you called to when you were freezing to death – we know you did that – we read the sign. You called to the wolf and the wolf came and saved you, well, for a short time maybe."

Then John Crow spoke.

"Let me cut you a deal HW – you lead us to the wolf and you can go free, no questions asked. I'll even throw in a few bucks for your trouble – how about a thousand dollars, does that sound good?"

The other Indians in the campsite were suddenly quiet – this was a lot of money, much more than they were being paid.

Hunter remained silent while entering his captured zone. His eyes glazed over and he refused to speak or move – he went 'into himself'. America had trained him well.

"OK, BOYS. STAKE HIM OUT!"

George Cohen ordered, and the Indians 'Whooped' their fearsome chant as they ripped his clothes off and laid him in a star shape on the snow-covered ground, some hundred yards away from their camp.

George Cohen went through his pockets and found a small wad of $200, all the money that Hunter possessed in the world. He also took out Mickey's precious Zippo. Hunter cursed himself – he should have left it with the cigarettes and whiskey.

"MT? That's not Michael Tomlin by any chance, HW? He's dead, but you know that donncha?"

Hunter controlled his anger and remained passive – he still had a lot of fight in him but had to wait for the moment.

They hammered in wooden stakes around his hands and feet until John Crow produced a large pot of hot water containing thin strips of rawhide leather.

They used this to bind his hands and feet tightly to the stakes, as they cooled, they would shrink. His clothes were left scattered all around, bait for the wolf.

Hunter accepted the process, he had no choice.

"If you won't take us to her HW, then she will come to you like she did before – you must be some special kind of wolf man."

Hunter remained silent as he felt the cold snow on his naked skin and the chords of leather being tied to his hands and ankles. He made a star shape on the ground and prayed to whatever God and Angels who were above to come and get him 'sooner than later please'. Unless the Angels gave him another moment, he clung on to the belief that they would.

Hunter was not afraid of dying; he should have been killed many times over in the past and half of him imagined that this would definitely be the end.

They left him alone for a short time while they drank whiskey around their camp fire which was at least a hundred yards away from where he was. He sensed the presence of two Indians waiting – waiting for her. So he 'said nothing', 'thought nothing', 'was nothing'

The sun began to go down as the now familiar cold arrived. Adrenalin had kept Hunter 'in the zone' but now he began to shake; after thirty minutes or so hypothermia would begin to set in. Before this happened, George Cohen and John Crow with the rest of the Indian's stood all around him.

"I guess I'm gonna have to make you call her, HW," George Cohen said holding Hunter's hunting knife in his hand.

"Mighty sharp weapon, HW."

The Indian looked Hunter over and suddenly noticed his two blackened toes.

"Oh, looky here, HW, you have frost-bitten toes – let me help you out here."

With that, the Indian knelt down at Hunters feet and in one swift slice took off the little toe on his right foot. Strangely enough, Hunter didn't feel a thing, the wound didn't even bleed. The Indian prodded around his big toe on the same foot, that was slightly blackened. Now this would hurt, Hunter thought to himself remaining unmoved. The Indian played with the toe causing Hunter a massive amount of pain.

"I'm gonna let you keep this one, HW. I know how much it must be hurting you."

He then moved to Hunter's other foot and cut off his other little toe, this time in a slow slicing movement. Thankfully this one was also numb.

George Cohen smiled at him sadistically.

"That didn't hurt you HW? This will – I can guarantee you that."

Then he stood up and took the blade to Hunter's chest.

He made a one inch cut a little way above Hunters left nipple then two horizontal cuts on either side and a final cut at the bottom. He knew what was coming; he was going to be skinned alive.

Using the sharp tip of the knife, the Indian lifted a corner piece of skin and began to pull it slowly away from the living flesh of Hunters chest. He had felt pain before but even the Viet Cong couldn't match this torture. He sniffed loudly trying to control himself, until the skin pulling stopped.

"Oh, you're a hard man, HW, but you ain't gonna die just yet."

With that, George Cohen threw a huge bearskin rug over Hunter's body. Immediately, he felt the warmth from the rug and realised that he would be alive for just a little bit longer.

Thirty minutes later someone removed the bearskin and let him freeze for a short while before George Cohen repeated the process on the right side of his chest. Hunter knew what to expect this time and showed even less reaction to the pain.

They carried on the procedure, each time taking off little slivers of skin before going back to their camp to drink whiskey.

The fifth time George Cohen cut him Hunter observed that the Indian could not even cut a straight line on his belly skin. 'Too much whiskey', Hunter thought. It was getting late now and he wondered if the stories about these Indians were true, especially the one that said, they didn't fight at night.

They left one of their young cousins armed with a hunting rifle to cover up Hunter with the bearskin rug, but he had drunk too much and just decided to sit with Hunter to tell him his own sad life story before falling asleep mid-sentence, still sitting upright but, completely passed out.

The snow began to fall heavily now landing on Hunter's shivering skin; he had lost all feeling in his hands and feet due to the constriction of the leather binding and now he desired the feeling of the large bearskin cover. He tried to connect with the boy who slept next to him but it was hopeless. Just at that moment, he closed his eyes and decided to die.

He had completed his mission and now he was going to find Mickey. Wherever Mickey was, he would find him.

He felt the bearskin cover him, heavier this time but then his scant sense of smell sensed the she-wolf laying on top of him once again.

She had licked at his bloody chest wounds before covering his naked torso with her hairy body.

"It's gonna take a bit more than you this time, girl," he whispered in her ear shivering as he did.

"Trust me, human."

Another wolf then laid itself along his right arm – one covered his left, and another two covered his legs. Whether it was the smell or taste of the leather he didn't know or care, the four wolves began silently chewing at his bonds and at the same time warming him with a natural blanket of wolf, just like before.

The Indian who had fallen asleep looked for a more comfortable position in his deep sleep and rested his head on the shoulder of Winter whilst snoring loudly. Hunter's frozen face smiled wildly at this irony and he began a silent giggle.

"Oh, shut up, human! I'm trying to save you."

Hunter's right hand became free and he eased it away from the Timber wolf who carried on chewing the leather; then his left hand which was underneath the sleeping Indian. Winter got up silently and Hunter managed to pull over the huge bear skin rug to put underneath the sleeping Indian's head replacing the comfort of Winter with this.

The rest of his bonds were chewed through and he was free. Silently, he gathered up his scattered clothing and dressed himself as best as he could. Mickey's oversized thermals were a God send and he immediately felt the warmth from them. He struggled with his pants and top not being able to fix any zipper or buttons with his frozen fingers but then his boots fitted easily now due to his loss of little toes.

Gently he wrapped the Indian in the huge bear skin rug and he began to snore even louder which was a comfort to him.

Hunter then took charge of the hunting rifle, expecting to make an escape with the wolves but then looked towards Winter who seemed relaxed and in fact, made herself comfortable on the ground. He sat beside her and whispered into her ear, "What's happening, girl?" before the other four wolves also joined in the family huddle, sharing their warmth with him.

Hunter held his frozen hands underneath his armpits to get back some more feeling before looking around at his new companions who refused to make eye contact with him.

"Hi, guys," he murmured.

"Don't talk to them!"

He looked further around and noticed black shadows moving past their huddle, silently in the night heading towards the Indian camp, many of them.

Hunter thought that he had seen most things in warfare and nothing would ever surprise him, but watching a whole pack of wolves silently surrounding a heavily armed Indian campsite blew him away completely. This was not the world according to Hunter; he was a privileged observer who would help as best as he could. He reckoned that the hunting rifle contained one bullet and more ammo was probably with the sleeping Indian in front of him who he did not want to disturb. The only weapon he really desired was 100 yards away – Mickey's M16A1. He watched as the wolves positioned themselves and guessed that they would attack at dawn.

The wolves waited patiently all night and the first to sense danger was the massive wolf hound 'Jet', who rose just before the sun came up.

He nervously sniffed the air around him before looking around at the rest of the Indians in their sleeping bags. He was not a coward, just a sensible dog. Slowly he made his way out of the camp towards the familiar track that he knew, watched by the wolves, who let him pass. Once reaching the track that led home, he took off like a racehorse in a sprint.

The she-wolf and her companions got up suddenly as one and headed into position, leaving Hunter alone with the Indian who was beginning to stir.

A high-pitched whistling sound came from the camp, "JET," said the Indian, who had captured Hunter called for his dog.

This woke the Indian still wrapped in the bearskin rug. Hunter then slammed the rifle butt onto his head.

"You go back to sleep, boy!" he whispered dryly before rummaging around his pockets, taking out a handful of rounds.

Hunter then took charge of the bearskin rug and wrapped it around himself.

The Indian calling his dog put two fingers in his mouth and as he took a deep breath to whistle once again, a wolf flew through the air and took his wrist in its jaws; a split second later another ripped into his ear and between them dragged the man to the floor.

The sound of almost 40 snarling wolves filled the air as they attacked the Indians from all sides, most of them still huddled in their sleeping bags.

Shots rang out from a Colt45 – Hunter's cowboy weapon that George Cohen had gifted to one of his cousins. Two of the timber wolves went down before Hunter shot him in the chest. This time he was shooting to kill.

He expertly reloaded the single shot weapon and looked for another target.

Every Indian that picked up a weapon was shot dead by Hunter.

George Cohen tried to pick up the M16A1 leant against a tree but a timber wolf flew through the air and held on to his upper arm. He managed to grasp the large hunting knife but then Winter grabbed his wrist causing him to drop the weapon. She released her grip and picked up the knife before heading back towards Hunter. He had taken station about 50 yards out shooting anyone that dared pick up a weapon. The Indians began to run, chased by the wolves. John Crow was fighting them off with a large tree branch. Hunter let him live, mainly just to watch him struggle. A wolf got him by the ankle and he went down, others taking chunks out of his arms and face.

Winter arrived at Hunter's side and dropped the hunting knife at his feet.

"Go on, beast – make a fire and warm yourself."

"Not now, girl – I'm pretty busy at the moment," Hunter said as he shot another Indian attempting to grasp a weapon.

She sniffed at the bearskin and stared at him with an indignant look.

"First you are a dragon, then a wolf and now you desire to be a dead bear – you really do confuse me, human."

The battle raged for only another few minutes until silence reigned.

None of the wolves actually killed a man this morning – only Hunter. They had savaged most of the Indians who had ran off and when Hunter walked into the aftermath of the battle, only George Cohen and John Crow remained, blooded and laid on the ground together with the leader of the timber wolves, snarling a warning close to both their faces. He then turned to Hunter and gave him an equally chilling warning before raising his head into the air, "*AHOOOooooooo*," calling his pack.

The pack all gathered around the campsite searching for danger but they had all gone. The pack leader then turned to Winter who crouched down on all fours in submission. Hunter noticed this and dropped the rifle and bearskin from his shoulders before he assumed the same position alongside her with his head bowed lowly. The leader snarled viciously at their faces without biting. Hunter surmised that in wolf terms, they were receiving a damned good telling off!

Then the whole pack left, following their leader, trotting out of the camp making loud little, "Yelps" between themselves – all happy and victorious.

This left Hunter and Winter alone with George Cohen and John Crow who were both bleeding heavily from their wounds. She guarded the Indians the same way as the wolf hound had threatened Hunter the day before. "Is that her, HW?" John Crow asked, trying to stem the flow of blood coming from his ankle and heavy wounds to his face.

"Uhu."

Hunter answered simply before picking up Mikey's M16A1 with the huge long sights and the rucksack that still contained some emergency rations along with 6 clips of ammo. The Indians had ripped apart everything he had owned and along with Mickey's Zippo, his last $200 dollars that had been in his Levi jeans pocket.

He retrieved the Colt45 from the hand of a dead Indian and took off his army-issued wrist watch from the same body. Hunter then put revolver into the rucksack along with the holster that had been left to one side before reattaching the watch to his wrist.

"I ain't never seen a wolf with that colouring before – looks like a dog wolf; that's why them timber wolves don't want her."

With that the she-wolf moved forward and snarled directly into the face of John Crow.

"Is this wolf enough for you?"

"More wolf than dog," he said repentantly spitting out blood from his mouth as he spoke.

Hunter then made that split-second eye contact with Winter who responded in kind.

"I guess you're coming home with me, girl," he thought silently.

"Where on this earth is that?"

Hunter then removed the Russian sights from Mickey's M16A1, a procedure that he had watched many times in the past but this was the first time that he had been allowed to do it.

The two Chippewa brothers watched as he turned the butterfly nuts two and a half times each anticlockwise before the sights dropped into his hand. Hunter amazed himself – Mickey had got this procedure down to 13 seconds and Hunter reckoned that he wasn't far away from this mark.

He deposited them into the rucksack. In a second, he unclipped the magazine, checked it for rounds, then clicked it back into place.

"It shoots high, doesn't it," George Cohen stated as Hunter held Mickey's precious gun in his hands once again.

"Not when I'm holding it," Hunter replied pointing the weapon at the head of the Indian who froze at this comment.

"You have something else of mine," Hunter said angrily to George Cohen who at this point wondered why he and his brother were still alive in the company of this deadly little man and his wolf.

Due to the lacerations all along his right arm, George Cohen had to use his left arm to reach into his pocket to retrieve the $200 dollars that were wrapped around Mickey's Zippo and throw the items to Hunter…

"Obliged," Hunter answered before leaving the area now heading due south.

"Lot of people will be coming after you!" he heard in the distance.

"Yea I know," he shouted back.

"All the way to Arizona!"

"Yea I know," he thought to himself.

Hunter had not even thought about getting as far as the desert farm back home and with the Indians comment, it dawned on him that he was now back in a war. They may have won the first battle, but there was more to come, much more!

***

36 hours later, Hunter and Winter were hidden in the forest looking out to the road and the entrance to the trailer park where he had parked his refrigerator wagon. During the few stops they had made to rest and eat some emergency rations, Hunter had offered shelter with the bearskin rug that he was still wearing around his shoulders, but she had declined.

"I need you, human, but you smell like a dead bear."

Using the Russian sights, he saw many comings and goings from the office until the early hours of the morning.

The lights were still on and Hunter was sure that the Indian manager was alone.

The snow had abated for a while and all was very quiet as they crossed the road and headed to the cabin. Both Hunter and Winter had checked out the whole area and were sure it was clear.

This time he walked directly into the office pointing his Colt45 at the shocked Indian's face, double-shocked to see the huge wolf follow him in.

He raised his hands in the air and Hunter in one fluid movement put down his weapon and began binding the man with the roll of sellotape from a holder that he had noticed on his previous visit. Hunter was an expert at this. When they 'snatched' Viet Cong soldiers back in Vietnam, they used tape to bind their victims.

Within seconds, the Indian had his arms secured behind his back and his mouth tapped over, sat down in his swivel chair.

He then looked over the key box to locate the refrigerator wagons keys but couldn't find them.

Hunter then beckoned to his partner with a sideways nod of his head.

She silently clamped her jaws around the Indians thigh and began to squeeze slowly, her sadistic eyes watching his as she gradually increased every ounce of pressure.

He began to panic and with his eyes pointed to one of the draws behind his desk.

Hunter opened the draw and found two sets of keys. One for his wagon and the other set he picked up anyway.

Hunter and Winter marched the man towards their wagon and from 50 yards away, they spotted a familiar vehicle, a large black ATV with blacked out windows and a red square that held a white cross, alongside the number plate, parked right next to them…

***

George Cohen and John Crow somehow managed to patch themselves up from the camp and with the help of some cousins eventually made it back to the trailer park at Lily and their vehicle. The office lights were still on when they got there but no one was in attendance.

George Cohen went in and retrieved the keys for the ATV from the desk draw before helping his limping brother towards their vehicle. The key opened the rear passenger door and as he pulled it back to let his wounded brother sit in the back seat, he found a bound-up cousin with a claymore mine resting between his legs.

'One thousand and one, one thousand and two'…
'BOOM!'

The car exploded in a mighty roar killing all the Indians in the vicinity. As the smoke from the ordinance blew away, hundreds of dollars drifted down to the snow-covered ground. It wasn't all of the bounty money. Hunter had at least $8,000 in his rucksack and was now getting the hell out of Langdale county.

***

Hunter needed a new ride. The refrigeration truck had served its purpose and was now a problem – it was a marked vehicle. He had to find something new. Hunter and Winter had driven solid for six hours only stopping to refuel, this time without incident. All across Wisconsin and half way across Minnesota, all the time thinking and planning.

Now that lack of money was not a problem, he could finally indulge himself in one of his dream rides – a VW camper van.

All the anti-Vietnam people in the news film clips that he had seen during the war drove colourfully painted VW vans; he wanted one for the pure irony. He would not stop until he found one.

Hunter also needed medical attention as his chest and belly wounds were beginning to hurt badly along with the pain of his frost-bitten big toe. His chest wounds chaffed against Mickey's thermal vest which was thankfully made of smooth, closely woven cotton but he knew the risk of infection was rising by the hour. He was still on a high and that was the only thing keeping him going.

In the early hours they had crossed the Stateline into Minnesota. As Hunter looked up to the sign indicating the crossing, he felt a small sense of relief of being away from the carnage of Wisconsin and so relaxed slightly.

"Made it out, girl," he spoke to the wolf who looked up to him puzzled.

"Out where?"

It was a full four hours before Hunter found what he had been looking for. They passed a roadside car lot and there she was, a brand new dark green VW camper van – bargain of the month at $2,800. The green colour reminded him of his military uniform and completed the irony.

"Check it out, girl – that is our new vehicle."

She just ignored this as she did whenever he muttered something unintelligible.

They now had to find somewhere to dump the refrigerator wagon so that it could not be connected to the new purchase.

A couple of miles further up the road and on the very edge of the small town, they passed a steakhouse/bar with a huge welcoming sign, 'Sweet Home Chicargo' at the entrance.

It was a sizable building all on its own with a vast parking area. Vehicles of all shapes and sizes were parked randomly around the dirt surface. "Left by guys who got so drunk, they had called a taxi home and then next morning forgotten where they left their rides," Hunter surmised. He turned the wagon around and pulled into the establishment hoping that no one was awake at this early hour. Picking a spot in between two other commercial looking trucks, he quickly parked up the wagon and switched off the engine. Looking at the dirty windows and bodywork of these vehicles next to them guessed that they hadn't been driven for some time. Quietly getting out, he opened up the passenger door to let the wolf out for her personal business and gave her a look,

"Don't you go too far, girl."

"Where can I go?"

After taking a short look around and urinating against the wheel of the truck next to them, she came back to the wagon and looked towards Hunter before leaping back to her seat. Hunter took off the number plates of the refrigerator wagon and replaced them with ones from a dirty looking pickup close by that he reckoned had not been driven for some time. The original plates he hid underneath another larger commercial truck. The effort made him sit for a while. He was getting tired, even Hunter had a 'max' and he was beginning to max out; only natural adrenaline kept had him going and that was now in short supply.

"This place is awful; can we go now?"

"We can't go yet, girl, I have to do a piece of business – few hours and we'll be on our way."

She stretched out on the seat with a look on her face like a bored child on a long journey.

"Oh, do we have to."

"Do you want to eat something?" Hunter asked rummaging thru the remaining emergency rations in his rucksack.

"All we have left is Cajun chicken and I must warn you that this does make me fart real bad."

She got up smelling the food as Hunter ripped off the top of the ration pack. A wolf is always hungry – they never know when the next meal is coming. Snatching the thing from Hunter's hands she sucked at the open top of the ration pack and pressed with her paws to extract the contents until it was empty before discarding the empty packaging into the foot well.

Hunter stared at her and opened up a second, to which she again snatched out of his hand, repeating her bullying process.

Hunter for the first time gave her an angry glare.

"Don't I get any?"

"No, you don't – you said you didn't like it."

Hunter gave her an angry face and growled towards her also for the first time.

The wolf simply moved her head forward and gave Hunter a massive lick of tongue-coated Cajun chicken, from his chin right up to his forehead. Hunter coughed and spat out the disgusting memory before smiling to himself, "Yea, that's exactly what I used to do to Mickey."

He then closed his eyes for a customary two-hour sleep.

One hour and 59 minutes into his nap, a sweet sickening odour woke him up.

"Aw man! you've just farted, haven't you? And that's a Cajun chicken fart! Before you girl, there was only one animal alive in this world that could achieve that amount of grossness – that was me!"

Franticly winding down his driver's window, he looked over to the wolf who had a pleased-with-herself look on her face.

"You nearly made me ill then, girl and I have only ever been that way once before in my life. Shall I tell you about it?"

"You are going to anyway."

"Yea, we were in the field, awaiting extraction and those damn air cavalry guys were two days late – emergency rations all gone and we were starving. I went for a hunt in the jungle and found a huge mushroom. I ate the whole thing myself and after two minutes, I sicked it all up – do you know what I did then?"

"Go on!"

"I picked it all up and ate it again. Hey, made me feel like I had two meals that day, girl!"

"Good for you!"

Hunter and the wolf's thoughts were interrupted by the loud sounds of motorbikes entering the parking lot. He recognised the unmistakable sounds of Harley Davidson engines – lots of them.

The wolf also sensed this and became agitated.

"So OK, girl. If they don't bother us, we won't hurt them, OK?"

"Hurt them? What does that mean?"

She just gave him the sideways look that she had when she sensed danger, or maybe something else.

Hunter left the wagon and watched as the bikers parked up and went into the bar. They were all pretty quiet and one of them who had been a pillion passenger was carried in hurriedly. Hunter could see the new blood stains on his black leather jacket. There must have been some trouble.

"OK, girl, I have to go out for a couple of hours now – you gonna be OK here?"

"Just do what you have to do, human."

Hunter stuffed $4,000 into his pockets from his stash in Mickey's old rucksack and looked towards his partner who stared back in understanding.

Hunter left the vehicle leaving the door slightly ajar – she could get out if she wanted to.

"Don't bother, human."

She then grabbed the door handle with her teeth and closed it after he had left before settling down for another short sleep.

Avoiding the main entrance to the parking lot where he could have been seen by the people in the bar, he made his way east down the main road. He walked quickly although hobbling like a person with bad feet which in fact he was. His new mission spurned him on the same as if he was walking through the Nicolet forests, but this time the added pain from his chest and stomach became a bigger burden. He would have to seek medical advice sooner than later.

Hunter arrived at the car plot and walked straight to the dark green VW camper van to begin lovingly stroking the vehicle. All he could smell was 'brand new, brand new'; he even sniffed the tires and caressed the chrome fender before a smiling salesman finally arrived at the scene. Three of them had spotted Hunter looking around the vehicle and they all drew lots for 'who is gonna deal with the mad crazy bum?'

"You like this vehicle I can tell, sir. Isn't she beautiful, hasn't she just got the b..."

"Sold! How much for cash?"

The car salesman was shocked; this wasn't how it normally happened but he had already worked out his cash sale commission for selling this vehicle.

"We're selling this model for $2,800. It's called the T25 Westphalia Joker and you have to agree that it's a fine..."

"$2,500 cash and I drive the thing away?" Hunter ordered looking at the now shocked salesman.

"Would you like to step into our office, sir and we could sort out the paperwork right away?"

Hunter beckoned the sales man to open the side door of the VW and showed him a carefully counted bundle of bank notes that he laid on the floor of the camper van.

"$3,000 and 'you' do the paperwork."

"I think we have an arrangement, sir. If you don't mind waiting for a moment, I'll just go and get you the key."

"And the log book," Hunter demanded.

"But, sir, of course! What name would you like on the document?"

"John Wayne," Hunter answered quickly; it was the first name that came into his head.

The car salesman walked past his colleagues striking a gay pose, hand on one hip and pointing his tongue out toward them as they sat in disbelief.

"Looks aren't everything, boys!" he smugly announced waving the massive wad of dollars.

The salesman wrote out the false paperwork and eventually came back handing the logbook to Hunter advising as he did.

"I've actually called you 'John Payne', sir. I think you'll understand why."

Hunter nodded gratefully as the irony built – he was in indeed in pain. Also, the name 'John Wayne' would have brought attention to him if he was ever to be stopped by any sort of authority.

Hunter drove out of the car sales lot and a half a mile down the road, drove into a gas station to fill up; he was reaching his point of total exhaustion.

"Fill her up, sir?" the young smiling attendant asked.

"Yea, dude," Hunter replied casually.

He walked into the petrol station shop and wandered around picking up his propensities – mainly bandages and some salve for his open wounds. Up until this time he had controlled the pain but he knew he would need some professional help soon.

"Damned Hell's Angels, why are they here?" Hunter heard from a guy at the counter talking to the cashier. "Shame all of them didn't get shot."

He was a big man, middle-aged working guy, very strong, lacking in skill and abundant with his mouth, Hunter surmised.

Hunter approached the desk and the conversation went quiet.

He paid for the items which included cigarettes and wanted to leave without incident but the man who had been talking to the cashier stood in front of him blocking his exit.

"Are you one of them sons of bitches?"

"No, sir. I can assure you that I am just passing through this town on my own," Hunter answered politely he didn't have much more to give at this point; well, maybe just one more fight.

"Well, you sure smell like one of them! You stink boy! You and your friends are going to be cleaned up real soon!"

Hunter didn't mind anyone tell him he 'stunk'; he knew it was probably the truth, but to be referred to as boy! Now that crossed the red line.

Hunter took two steps towards the man and without breaking stride, simply kicked the big guy between his legs before spinning around and delivering a heavy karate stamp kick to one side of his right knee. The big oaf fell into a display of baked bean cans along with a now dislocated kneecap.

"You'll have to help him up," Hunter advised the shocked young man behind the counter before leaving. Hunter walked onto the gas station forecourt pulling $100 dollars from his wad of money.

The young attendant smiled again as he approached but then hardened as he saw the look on Hunter's face.

"Twenty for the gas, forty for you, forty for your friend inside – you did not see me, you did not see my ride – have a nice life."

As he drove the VW out of the gas station, Hunter wickedly thought to himself.

"Man, I've just promoted myself from special forces to the CIA."

It was only a short ride back to the bar and Hunter figured that there must be some local dispute happening between the bikers and the locals. He also knew the difference between bikers and Hell's Angels; it was a bit like being regular army or special forces. Either way, he didn't like them in their similar-styled leather jackets. If they want to wear a uniform, they should join the US Army, was Hunter's attitude.

He pulled into the bar's parking lot and stopped a little way from the fridge wagon; the light was fading now and Hunter thought – a quick transfer of goods – mainly the wolf, rucksack and weapons stored in the back of the vehicle, then off. He grimaced as he got out of the VW. He had kicked the guy with his bad foot and now it was really beginning to hurt – even more so than his skin-stripped chest.

Hunter transferred the rucksack and the weapons before hiding the rest of the cash behind the dashboard of the new VW. The wolf was nowhere to be seen. Hunter stopped for a moment and smoked a Marlborough from a pack that he had bought in the gas station. Mickey's two-year-old cigarettes had tortured his lungs and this particular smoke was sweet, very sweet.

"Maybe I should just leave her here?" he thought for a split second but, "nah, that would kill me for the rest of my life. I don't leave anyone – she's out there somewhere."

The strains of Lynard Skynard's song *Freebird's* long intro sucked his attention towards the bar. It had begun quietly but then the volume suddenly increased. He had to go, as tired as he was.

The song carried on as he walked up to the bar, feeling the eyes of the people inside but trying to be nonchalant until his well-trained eye noticed that there were only bikers in the bar.

Hunter found himself in between two huge leather-clad men who made a space for him and a big, black lady behind the bar spoke directly to him.

"I ain't even gonna ask what you want, mister. I can see it in your face – I can see that the lord wishes to give you a Jamaican rum, and I'm sorry if it's a large one, it's just the way its gonna have to be."

"Oh, let the Lord be right, Mother!" Hunter answered her directly.

She gave a shocked look on her face before singing back the reply.

"Let the heavens be praised!" she sang in loud Gospel.

"Let the light shine on the holy ones," Hunter responded.

"Then we all be safe and saved!" she ended with a flourish.

Only Hunter and the big, black lady knew what they were singing about. Two men from his team back in Vietnam were black guys, Edwin and Louis, both from South Carolina and whenever there had been an important decision to be made, they always sang this between themselves to pray for the correct outcome. After a couple of difficult missions, the whole team would sing this gospel tune together in times of stress.

She gave her OK sign to the bikers.

Hunter looked left and then right – they had stopped looking at him so he just paid the dollar for the drink; after all, the eight-minute guitar solo was just coming up.

By the end of the solo, hunter's glass was empty and before he could replenish his drink, the big guy on his left asked,

"Why are you here, mister?"

"I'm looking for my dog – she go out," Hunter answered quickly, now unsteady on his feet.

The big guy looked down at him interested and said,

"We'll cut you a deal, mister – you buy everyone here a drink and we'll tell you where your dog is."

Hunter looked up at him and smiled.

"I think my dog can take care of herself, but if you guys want a drink, sure thing! Hey can we have some service here lady?"

Hunter pulled another hundred-dollar roll from his back pocket and placed it on to the counter, "Drinks all around and have a big one for yourself."

He was having an 'easy come, easy go' moment and when the sound of his favourite Marcus Malone song – *'Complications'* – blasted out from the juke box, he felt elated.

Knocking back his new large Jamaican rum in one go, he turned to the big biker on his left who then watched Hunter's eyes roll back before he collapsed to the floor. He had finally reached his point of no return, totally exhausted, in pain and pretty sick.

"Hey where's 'Doc' at?" the big guy shouted at the rest of the gang.

"Just coming out of the bathroom, Jez," one replied.

A bespeckled biker made his way to the prone hunter and felt the heat on his forehead. He had done five years of medical college and was six months away from qualifying for full doctor, before giving everything up to run away with a biker gang and live life on the open road. That had been two years previously and his wealthy parents had not spoken to him since.

"Yea he's sick. Can we get him somewhere that I could have a closer look at him Betty?" he asked the big, black lady who owned the bar.

"You'll have to put him up with Phil. I guess you guys are gonna have the rest of the rooms."

Doc nodded knowingly. Phil was the wounded biker that Hunter had noticed being carried into the establishment, bleeding heavily.

One of the big bikers easily picked up Hunter and took him up the stairs to a small room.

"He's only small but there's a funny smell about this guy; smelt it before but I just can't put my nose on it."

The Doc followed carrying a leather medical bag, Betty the owner of the place opened the door before gently wrapping up the body of Phil in the blankets he was laid on and with the help of Doc, placed the body on the floor before the big guy put Hunter on the bed.

Doc set about his work. Hunter was running a very high temperature. He could tell this without the use of a thermometer and set about finding the reason. Hunter groaned in his sleep as the Doc ran his hands over his chest.

Lifting up the bottom of his upper shirt and Mickey's thermal vest, he exposed Hunter's belly wounds, red and raw.

"Oh my God, Jez – check this out!"

The big biker looked at the mess of mutilated skin – he had heard about this but had never seen it first-hand.

Doc cut away the vest that was sticking to the rest of his wounds to expose the whole horror of his chest and belly.

"Hot water and some usable towels please, Betty – this needs cleaning up badly."

"What the hell happened to him?" she shouted on her way out of the room.

"Indians got him, Betty – he's been skinned alive. See this here – they must have bound him up with rawhide."

Jez, the big biker, answered noticing the dark red marks around his wrists and guessed there would be the same marks around his ankles.

"Injuns? This is 1978, Jez. It ain't 1878," Betty said feeling sick from the sight as she left to get the hot water and towels.

Jez noticed the top three perfectly cut, two-inch by one-inch cuts of skin; the lower they got, the less symmetrical they were.

"Aw man, this guy has been seriously cut, but look at this – the bottom ones are wobbly, probably done by a drunk Indian – can't think of anything worse."

Jez would know, he was part Yankton Sioux himself.

His mother was from Sweden originally hence his long mane of blond hair but he still had the dark eyes of a Sioux warrior.

Betty arrived back with a bucket of hot water and some old tea towels.

"Is this the best you can do, Betty?" Doc said looking at the unhygienic items.

"You work with it, Doc, it's all I can spare. I put some salt in the water if that helps."

"Yea man, looks like he can put up with some pain," Jez followed.

Doc raised his eyes but then began the long process of cleaning Hunter's wounds.

"Make a call, Jez; he's gonna need penicillin. I'm nearly out."

"Sure thing, Doc. I guess the little guy has money – he can pay us later."

Doc just waved him away.

"Busy day, eh Doc? Shame about Phil."

"The sniper shot him through his back, punctured both his lungs. I couldn't save him."

Jez and Betty left the Doc to his work and went back down to the bar.

Doc carried on with Hunter and gave him a thorough check over, taking off his boots and slipping his pants off; he couldn't find any problems. He was working from top to bottom. If he had been tortured even more than he had been, they would have attacked the genitals surely, but, no problems there. The moment Doc took off Hunter's socks however he knew the problem. Frostbite and a possibility of gangrene. The wounds he had cleaned were new and would heal with his help but this had been going on for some time. Doc prodded around the two small toes that Hunter had lost; they looked pretty cauterised and would heal naturally but the big toe on his right foot was half and half – it would be better if the blackened top half of the toe was removed so that the bottom half could heal. The danger of gangrene setting in was a possibility. This one the Chippewa Indian had played with somehow knowing the same thing. He touched it and Hunter moaned in his sleep.

"Give me some help here!" Doc called out.

The sound of running feet on the wooden stairs filled the air and then two bikers entered the room.

"Hold him."

"He's asleep, Doc."

"Hold him," Doc ordered again.

The young Doc prepared himself for some emergency surgery, picking out items from his medical kit that were brand-new and as yet unused. He had studied amputations during his years at medical college but this would be the first time he would had performed an operation. He looked at his wrist watch before beginning.

Two bikers held Hunter tight as the Doc cut around his bad big toe with a scalpel, peeling the good skin down before he made the final cut. With a small medical saw, he took off the top half of the damaged toe. He had fixed a tourniquet just below Hunter's right knee but blood still squirted over his face as he cut through the bone. Eventually the bad top of Hunter's toe dropped onto the bed and then onto the floor so that the Doc could control the loss of blood from the small stump. When the flow of blood eventually subsided, he wrapped the good skin back around what was left of the digit and sewed it together. Then, being quite pleased with his knit work, bandaged up Hunter's foot along with dressings for his chest and belly wounds.

Doc had been taking glances at his watch all this time. It was one hour and 58 minutes since Hunter had collapsed in the bar and he wondered if his prediction was going to be correct.

"It's OK, guys, you can go back to the bar now."

He then took out a file of morphine and pushed the whole thing into Hunter's left bum cheek. He seemed unmoved by the drugs but then on the stroke of two hours, Hunter's eyes opened madly and then closed quickly with the effects of the morphine.

Doc was studying his watch and made the comment.

"Yep, just like my dad."

He then gave Hunter an injection of penicillin in his other bum cheek before sitting on one of the comfortable chairs in the room to watch over his patient, his face and hands still covered with Hunter's blood.

***

Two large and obviously gay men took charge of the bar from Betty – this is what 'Sweet Home Chicargo' was all about. It was somewhere anyone could go to and have a good time and that's what the good people of the town didn't like. Betty's work didn't stop there; she went to open up the kitchen and get the grill heated up – she cooked the best steaks for miles around.

She had welcomed the bikers as inhouse security, a year ago after some of the locals had begun taking liberties –

helping themselves to the beer and spirits behind the bar. Betty was a big capable woman but she was on her own. Jez and his gang were quite a fearsome bunch but Hunter was correct in his 'biker' description of them. Jez especially did not want to be subjected to the strict rules of the 'Hell's Angels' who demanded lifelong loyalty and insisted on all sorts of initiations and tests which included having your jeans urinated on by everyone in the gang and then wearing them when they'd dried out, stinking and unwashed – 'originals'. Even so, they were affiliated to the Northern USA Chapter of Hell's Angels and did their own share of running drugs around Minnesota – just weed and hash. Jez wasn't interested in heroin or the new kid on the block – cocaine. The Angels would call on them when they needed a show of force and the Jez gang of nearly 20 bikers would come to their aid. Jez was at the point of calling in a favour from the Angels or 'One Percenters' as they were also known as.

Things had become serious when they had been riding out – two of the gang had been killed when one of the bikes mysteriously exploded. That had been a few days ago, and now Phil.

They had been riding in open ground when he just seemed to fall off his bike. No shots were heard but everyone saw the obvious bullet wound before riding around the whole area trying to discover the source of the aggression but to no avail. Jez reckoned that some sort of professional killer was out to get them one by one and he needed help.

Hunter interested him – he wanted to talk to him before bringing in the One Percenters.

***

The wolf was by this time well-practiced at opening and shutting the door to the refrigerator wagon with her long toothy jaws, Hunter just hadn't noticed. A little while after Hunter had left, she sensed the all clear and left the vehicle, shutting the door behind her with her front paws. Hunter had cleverly parked at the edge of the parking lot which was bordered by a bank of earth, three feet high, which indicated the boundary for the whole establishment. The main road ran along the opposite side to where she was and the rest of the flat land around as far as you could see was a swathe of long grass. Grateful that the grass was tall enough to cover her movement, she went into the field and stealthily made her way around the whole area, checking it out, looking for an escape route from the parking lot – and of course, looking for food. After an hour of fruitless and monotonous searching, she heard the sound of a vehicle pulling into the car park and went to investigate. Sure enough, it was Hunter returning in the new vehicle.

She watched as he transferred the rucksack and weapons wrapped in blankets to the new home and was going to run to join him but suddenly sensed something different about the grass around her – it had been flattened. She sniffed around; a human had been lying there. She looked up to see Hunter smoking a cigarette and was going to call him before he walked into the bar but then took it upon herself to follow the trail of flattened grass as it curved around the outside edge of the parking lot. A crawling human had made this track. It ended at the main road where there was a layby surrounded by trees, just up from the entrance to the bar. She waited patiently sensing that something was not quite right about this, in the way that only a wolf would understand.

She was correct – a vehicle similar to the ones driven by the shooting party in Canada arrived and she saw one man inside looking around for danger – she knew he couldn't see her.

The wolf watched the man fuss about his equipment inside the cab. At one point she saw the end of a rifle and her anger rose but then she calmed as he left the vehicle carrying only a large pair of binoculars but wearing some strange clothes that made him look like grass. Now her anger began to rise to breaking point – flash memories of the recent past that she had locked away returned; men in the snow – dressed as snow.

It was almost dark now as she watched his careful movements, bending down to crawl as he reached the long grass beyond the trees. She waited some time before approaching the man's vehicle and sniffed around; luckily for him, it wasn't one she was familiar with but even so she urinated all over the driver's door, making sure she hit the door handle.

Stealthily following the pressed grass trail, she quickly caught up with the crawling human, hearing his efforts. At one point he stopped, himself sensing he was being followed. She stopped at the same time waiting for him to move again.

He did so and she let him go further before letting out the slightest of haunting growls.

The man stopped again and ripped off his camouflaged headdress, trying to hear more clearly.

The wolf was now in her most sadistic mode; she had no reason to hurt this human but she was going to scare the crap out of him for her own pleasure, if nothing else.

She let him reach his intended position and began observing the bar, before moving back into the long grass into another position away from where he was, before producing another haunting sound.

This time she heard nothing except for a small clicking sound, a weapon being armed. She decided on caution and silently made her way around the area until she picked up the man's flattened grass trail once again. Making sure he was still in his position, she deposited a huge dump of Cajun chicken scat in the middle of his trail.

If he didn't have a sense of smell, he would be in deep trouble. She took cover in the trees and waited. This was a wolf's warning and she wanted him to know whoever he was, that a wolf was on his tail. She waited patiently as he finally appeared, wiping his hand repeatedly on the grass and then finally opening up the door to his RV with his left hand, before reaching in to pick up a bottle of water that he opened and attempted to clean his hands. He then got the stink of the wolf's marker on his other hand. Grabbing a towel from inside the cab, he began to wipe his hands franticly.

She let out a long haunting quiet growl from where she was before disappearing back into the long grass. Job done. Hopefully he would never come back.

Hunter was finally allowed to wake up; he had never been wounded before and had never experienced the effects of morphine until this day, even though he had administered the drug many times to wounded comrades during the war.

"OK," he murmured to himself, "where am I now?"

He managed to sit up and found himself bound by bandages, all across his chest and stomach; he threw away the blanket covering his lower half and looked to his also-bandaged right foot. *Guess I still have a left foot and a couple of lucky hands*, Hunter thought to himself.

Looking down to the body wrapped in blankets on his left side of the bed, Hunter pulled away some of the covering to reveal a blue head with closed eyes and long black hair.

"I guess you've been in a war too buddy; give me your name so I can say some prayers for you."

"His name was Phil," the bespeckled biker replied to Hunter's question as he sat in the chair before getting up to check out his patient, his face and hands still stained with Hunter's blood, giving him a look similar to the painted Chippewa Indians.

"You cut my bad toe off?" Hunter asked warily.

"Yes, that was me."

"Much obliged to you, Doc – that had been bothering me for weeks."

"Why was that? Where have you been?"

Hunter watched as the Doc produced a huge needle and indicated to him to turn onto his belly and received the most painful jab in his rear bum cheek. Small as they were, they were the most precious parts of his body.

Hunter grimaced. He was not going to show any signs of pain even though, he thought it was just as painful as being skinned alive.

"It's the best way in for penicillin and that's what you need, you have septicaemia."

"Septa what?"

"Blood poisoning, and in your case, it was border line gangrene; that could have happened. You are lucky."

"I've never ever considered myself lucky, Doc," Hunter replied guessing that this young man had some medical experience.

"Yea right, but you remind me of my dad; he was in the same stupid war that you were in – idiots all of you"

The young Doc had been too young to experience the Vietnam War and because of his privileged upbringing would not have been drafted into the army. Mainly because of his father, he felt an absolute disgust for the war and anyone that had been involved in it.

"Stay loose, Junior – nobody wanted that war. How do you know I was in the army?"

The young Doc looked at him as if he had smelled a bad smell – he probably had.

"You smell of army, in fact you stink of army and your vehicle even looks like army. You have Vietnam veteran written all over your body and in your mind, as for your 'nobody wanted it comment', you are so wrong, mister, America wanted that war or it wanted 'a' war. Ho Chi Min loved America and wanted to ally his country with us, rather than the repressive state of the USSR at that time and even China. When America took over from the French in 1965, they didn't know what would happen and they did not even speak to Ho Chi Min. Arrogance, total arrogance! Johnson thought he could just walk into the country and wipe out the bad guys; well, you must have had one hell of a shock when you found out that you were the bad guys – that's why you lost and you damned well deserved to lose!"

Hunter thought for a while. This was a distinct lack of respect for himself and his fallen comrades and unlike his normal controlled self, his anger began to rise, albeit assisted by the drugs and the sight of Doc's blood-splattered face.

"Who was your dad?" Hunter questioned angrily in his drug-filled haze.

"You might have known of him – Colonel Bradbury – he was in charge of the Air Cavalry."

This sent Hunter over his edge.

Hunter went instantly into his anger trance upon hearing this information – even worse than seeing any politician on a TV screen. White noise filled his ears as in battle, as he looked towards the young man with mad eyes.

The young man noticed this rise in aggression and his next call probably saved his own life.

"JEZ!" Doc shouted once as Hunter grabbed him by the throat and began to squeeze.

The big Jez arrived in seconds and grabbed on to Hunter who let go of the Doc's throat before instinctively cocking his right thumb and hitting the big guy just below his chin with what appeared to be just a slight blow. Jez suddenly collapsed in a heap alongside his dead friend, Phil and thankfully two other bikers arrived to hold Hunter down. The Doc jabbed yet another file of morphine into Hunter and he eventually calmed.

Doc looked towards Jez, who remained unconscious for a few minutes. He had never ever seen anyone put this big guy down, let alone a little skinny guy, who was seriously ill.

Hunter went into a morphine-induced sleep as the Doc administered to Jez who eventually got up holding and rubbing his painful face.

"Aw man that hurt; this little guy has some serious skill – what is he, Doc?"

Doc was also rubbing his squashed throat and spoke hoarsely.

"Vietnam veteran, maybe special forces 'cause he knows and hate's my dad, that's for sure, and what is that smell Jez?"

He thought for a while; a smell that came from the past when he finally got it.

"Wolf, I got it now; took me a while to work out but that smell is wolf."

The young man nodded in agreement.

"He must be the guy on the news, the one from Canada where the wolf killed some woman and an American brought it across the border – did you see that?"

"Yea, and the little guy said he'd lost his dog, maybe he'd lost his wolf. He came in a fridge wagon – the one that's parked out there – then he went out and bought a VW camper wagon, that brand new green one," Jez advised knowingly; nothing was missed in this establishment.

"In which case the wolf must be with him, and it's probably here right now."

Jez rolled his eyes, before asking,

"So you want me to go out there and find a wolf?"

"Need all the help we can get right now and you are part Indian; you should know all about these things," Doc said quietly. Jez just took a deep breath and nodded. Doc was always right.

"Hey Doc, go wash your face and hands – you look like a zombie man," Jez advised the Doc before he walked down the stairs to the kitchen and looked towards Betty who was hard at work. The bar had filled and she had a full book of covers.

"Hey, Betty, give me a steak, 11oz rump ought to do."

"Sure thing, just wait in line and I'll get it for you. How do you want it – medium rare?"

"No, betty. I just want the steak, raw; it's for the little fella's dog."

Betty went into a spiral of shouting.

"You wanna feed one of my steaks to a dog!"

Jez nodded sympathetically.

Betty suddenly realised that this was important and searched around in the cooler before bringing out the best 28-day cured piece of raw beef that she could find.

"Still gonna cost you $2.50," she shouted to Jez before handing him the beautiful piece of raw meat wrapped in kitchen paper.

He was about to venture in the parking lot but his natural Indian instincts told him to beware.

Back tracking up the stairs to where Hunter was being looked over by Doc, who was now fast asleep on a chair, he picked up the remains of Mickey's thermal vest along with Hunter's dried blood and scent.

The wolf heard the sound of footsteps from 100 yards away; they were heading toward her, she could sense it. Expertly opening the door to the fridge wagon, she got out and gently closed the door shut before taking cover underneath one of the large, commercial, abandoned vehicles next to her.

Jez had to admit it to himself that he was pretty nervous as he walked through the dark parking lot towards the fridge wagon. This normally fearless huge man was walking into the unknown.

She saw him coming towards her holding both hands out as if in offering.

"Big human!" then raised her head slightly and sniffed.

"Big human, nervous sweat, my dragon human, meat!"

Jez looked around seeing nothing move before opening the door to the wagon and looking inside. The cab was empty, just an old blanket in the well but the smell was there – definitely wolf.

She positioned herself behind him and began with a low growl that rose to a fever pitch as she threatened him and then silence!

He was transfixed by fear for a moment and could not move.

After a short while, the big man slowly turned around but she had disappeared.

He placed the large raw steak onto the passenger seat, throwing the remains of Mickey's vest into the well of the wagon before shutting the door. At the same time the driver's door opened and the cabin light turned on as she leapt into the cab and stood above the meat that had been offered to her. She then stared straight into the face of the shocked Jez through the window of the now-closed passenger door.

He stared back at her amazed, looking into her big eyes hypnotised by this most revered creature until she blinked and began licking at the large chunk of raw meat.

After a moment she looked up once again and continued staring at him. "Are you still here?"

Jez walked back to the bar in a state of shock and ordered a large Woodford Reserve bourbon without ice and downed the drink in one gulp.

"Ooo, Jesmond, you are a thirsty little boy," Felix the totally camp bartender observed, hand on hip.

"Would you like another?"

Jez held out his hand and quietly requested, "Bottle."

Felix handed the curved shaped bottle to Jez without further comment.

Jez then joined the snoozing Doc upstairs and watched over Hunter for the next two hours.

The wolf tore into the steak and despatched the meat in four mouthfuls before venturing out into the cold dark night. She went directly for the new VW and tried both door handles finding them locked before returning to the fridge wagon, slightly confused and feeling alone. She remained awake worrying and waiting.

After his customary two-hour sleep, Hunter awoke and looked at the two figures asleep on chairs at the end of his bed. His hands had been gently tied to the head of the bed behind him with kitchen towels. Silently releasing himself, he sat up and surveyed the situation.

A young Doc asleep with a now clean face and a big fella asleep next to him, a half-drunk bottle of Woodford Reserve in one hand and a half-filled glass in the other. Hunter gently relieved the big fella Jez of the bottle and glass before topping himself up and taking a swig of the contents.

Jez and Doc awoke at the same time looking at the completely naked Hunter sitting upright on the side of the bed, sipping at the whiskey and staring at them.

Hunter broke the awkward silence.

"Hey guys, do you have any cigarettes? I seemed to have lost mine, along with everything else."

Jez pulled a pack of smokes from the top pocket of his leather jacket and offered one to Hunter before taking one himself.

Doc didn't smoke. He'd maybe have a 'puff' off someone's 'doobie' occasionally but that was about it. Jez lit the smokes with his own Zippo lighter.

"I found your dog, man – he's OK. He's hanging out in your fridge wagon – we fed him an all."

Hunter smiled knowing he'd made the same mistake.

"He's actually a 'she' dude, and she's kinda cute ain't she?"

The look on the big biker's face said it all, Hunter realised that he was telling the truth.

"Well thanks guys for fixing me up; just give me another butt jab with that stuff Doc and my clothes, then we'll be on our way – I'll pay you for the inconvenience."

"Ain't about the money, mister, what it you name anyhow? Whatever it is we can help you out here – everyone needs friends, we certainly need friends right now so maybe I want to ask you if we can help each other out?"

Doc spoke and Hunter realised that these guys were also in some sort of conflict. The chance meeting in the gas station with the big lump and the dead biker at the side of his bed spoke volumes – also he was worried about Ma. The Swiss guy whose one mission in life was to kill the wolf, and no doubt he was obviously pretty wealthy according to the amount of money he had paid the Chippewa, and the only lead he would have to him would be through her. He might need help to get Ma out of Gackle and set her up somewhere else – now that he had the money. The house was too big for her on her own. Mickey had always wanted to keep the family home but Ma had confided in Hunter numerous times telling him her true desire – a small house near a lake of water surrounded by a forest with lots of children nearby so she could hear them laugh and play.

"I have to make a call, can you get me some clothes here?"

Jez left the room and came back with a bright pink dressing gown stolen from Betty's room.

"We had to cut most of your clothes off you so just put this on for now – there's a phone booth in the bar."

Jez helped Hunter down the stairs to the bar area. He looked ridiculous in an oversized bright pink dressing gown.

"Am I slightly overdressed for this place?" Hunter asked.

"Don't worry, man, you will not look out of place in this establishment."

It was two in the morning and the bar was in full swing with what seemed like the whole gay community of Minnesota converging in this one bar, that's the sort of place it was.

Betty watched Jez help Hunter move towards the phone booth.

"Hey! He's wearing my dressing gown!"

Hunter closed the door of the almost-soundproof phone booth and pressed the numbers of Ma's home telephone and entered a dime when the call connected.

"Who is this and what do you want…?"

Ma answered before Hunter heard a click and silence…he then heard Ma half way through her next sentence.

"I'm sorry ma'am, I dialled the wrong number," Hunter replied before slamming the phone down quickly, knowing that Ma would have recognised his voice. Even though it was the early hours of the morning, he knew that Ma would be awake – she didn't sleep much either.

Her phone was being tapped – he would indeed need help.

***

Early on that day at 'Rosie's bar' in the middle of the town, a big man on crutches struggled with the outside doors until a waitress quickly came to his aid and held one open as he ungratefully brushed past her.

Sitting down heavily in the private booth opposite a lone man, she appeared quickly to take his order.

"Whiskey and what will you have? Pussy water?" he asked the man.

"Mineral water to give it its correct title – what happened to you?"

"Never you mind, just do what we're paying you for," the big man answered slipping a white envelope across the table.

"That's for three, how come it's not more? You should have wiped out the whole gang by now."

The man sat silently not wanting to answer the question. The timing device he had placed onto one of the bikes had been one thing, taking out two bikers had been just a lucky event. When he had shot the biker, it was a different scenario; had he made two shots he would have compromised his position, as it was, one of the searching bikes rode directly over his cleverly disguised hiding hole buried in the ground.

"Slowly, slowly, catchy monkey," the man said as he stood up to leave the bar.

"Hey don't people like you ever wash? You smell like dog shit mixed with piss man."

Even though the tall man had showered an hour before, try as he might, no amount of scrubbing would remove the smell of the Cajun chicken scat on one hand and a wolf's abrasive urine on the other. He decided at that moment that he would need help. He hadn't in his wildest dreams imagined that he would find himself up against a wolf.

"Hey and take out some of those dammed faggots – we need them gone too," the big lump shouted at him as he left the small bar.

As an afterthought the big guy added.

"Hey, if you see a little skinny guy – take him out too."

***

Hunter came out of the phone booth and grabbed hold of Jez's hand much to the amazement of the gay community in the bar. "Oh, Jesmond, you have a boyfriend; why wasn't it one of us you devious dyke!"

"Yea, kiss my arse, girls!" he shouted before he actually realised what he'd said,

"Oooo, can we?" they all shouted as one before he ushered the unsteady Hunter back up the stairs to the room.

Hunter smiled as he limped up the stairs, remembering a particular night in Saigon when he had enjoyed a rare night of 'RNR'.

Jez and Doc made Hunter comfortable on the bed. The body of Phil had been taken away – they were going to give him his send-off the next day.

Hunter sat with a large glass of Woodford Reserve smoking a Marlborough, still dressed in Betty's pink dressing gown, holding court to a large group of bikers headed by Jez and the Doc.

"So who's dogging you guys?" Hunter asked, always eager to learn information but not disclose any.

Doc spoke intelligently.

"It's a local problem I think – we have tried to keep ourselves to ourselves; just coming and going from Betty's, doing our business, minding our own. We stay away from them and up until this point they have stayed away from us. Two weeks ago, we were riding out, one of the 'Hogs' exploded, killing two of our friends. We're no experts but we think the bike had been rigged the night before. We looked over the wreckage the next day and found a couple of things that shouldn't have been there."

Doc opened up a supermarket bag and pulled out a small burnt, twisted box linked to some sort of timing device and handed it to Hunter, whose expert eye didn't notice much but his nose did.

"Yea man, that's Semtex or C4, plastic explosive, kind you see in those ridiculous English spy films. What's that guy's name? James Kong or something?" Hunter asked.

"That's James Bond," Doc informed him.

"Yea well you know, when you see the films, he has a little bit hidden underneath one of his finger nails and this piece manages to blow up the whole building! It ain't quite like that but to blow up one of your motorcycles, it wouldn't take an awful lot. You'd need the training to use it though and it's expensive stuff – not your buy-off-the-shelf sticks of dynamite."

They listened intently to Hunter before Doc carried on.

"Yesterday we were hit by a sniper, when we were riding out on open ground. We covered every inch of that place, half a mile square but found nothing; we didn't even hear the shot and you saw what happened to Phil."

"Oh, yea man, I prayed for his soul," Hunter replied drifting off into another place; morphine and Woodford Reserve whiskey were starting to mix together quite nicely – he felt no pain at all for the first time in weeks.

"So you would agree that the person or persons dogging us, as you would say, is probably a professional killer, hired by a person or persons in our town?"

"Apparently so," Hunter answered quickly.

"So how do we deal with this situation?"

"You kill it," Hunter said simply.

"So how would we even begin to know how to do that?"

Hunter lit a cigarette and began thinking hard. They all stared at him waiting for his response and after he'd finished the smoke, he stubbed out the butt and simply announced,

"I'll work on it…if you want me to?"

giving the bikers in the room a serious stare as they all nodded in agreement. He knew what to do already but he also needed help to rescue Ma from her predicament; his mind was working on that problem. Thinking of Mickey's Dragunov sights that they had taken from a dead Viet Cong sniper, Hunter had been the bait purely because he was so small and quick; he would have been a difficult target. The sniper had shot at him three times before his team finally got him. Mickey had fired the fatal shot so he had claimed the Dragunov sights as his reward.

Hunter thought that the bikers would all be the bait and that killing 'him' would not be a problem; he just had to find a killing ground and prepare the area carefully. Easy project.

Getting Ma out was not an easy project. Hunter had been surprised by the speed at which the Chippewa Indians had turned up at Ma's place. He knew that the only connection had been the logging of the pickup's number plate at the border crossing and there was only one organisation in America that could have given the Swiss guy this information so quickly, the FBI.

At about 3 am, Jez left the room to lock up the bar – one of their jobs as security. This left Doc and Hunter alone in the room. Remembering the last time he had mentioned his father, Doc nervously asked Hunter,

"Did you know my father?" keen to know something about him from somebody who had actually been there with him during the war.

Hunter thought for a second, the memory of getting violent was still a distant blur due to the drugs he had experienced but then it came back.

"I saw him, and I heard him," Hunter replied softly.

"Would he know you if I said your name?"

NOW THAT WAS A QUESTION!

Would the man who had sentenced Hunter to 3 years in a Vietnam prison even know who he was?

"Junior, my name is Hunter Wisekat, and you're old man left me behind, that's all there is to say on the matter."

Doc knew what this meant. His father had always felt guilty for the guys left behind – one of the few things he told his son after he had been drinking. Their conversation would always stop at this time as the old colonel did not want to cry in front of his son.

"Would you kill him, if you ever met him?"

Hunters mind went wild for a few seconds but then he grabbed hold of himself.

"No," was Hunter's simple answer; he was thinking that he'd probably punch him half to death but no, he would not kill him. It had been his own choice to stay as the rear guard. He had always hoped that there was a good reason for the helicopters not returning to pick him up.

"So Hunter, who's dogging you?" the young Doc asked.

"Ah you know, the usual people; a very affluent Swiss guy whose life's mission is to kill my girl and probably me, the FBI, and after recent events most of the Chippewa Indian tribe."

"What?!"

The young Doc blurted out. He thought for a moment before connecting some news reports.

"Chippewa Indians ravaged by a pack of wolves – Chippewa Indians blown up in a trailer park by some sort of gas explosion – that was you wasn't it?!" asked Doc chuckling knowingly.

Hunter gave him back an innocent look on his face, shrugging his shoulders.

"What's so funny, Junior?"

"Jez, Hunter, he is part Yankton Sioux – he hates the Chippewa or Ojibwa as he calls them; they stole all their tribes land, the Yankton have a small reservation in South Dakota, they should have had more. I know he likes you Hunter, now he is going to love you and your wolf."

With that, the doors downstairs closed with a bang and Hunter heard the slightest footprints on the stairs before the big sound of Jez walking up.

Jez put his big blond covered head around the door announcing.

"Hey, mister, we found your dog!"

She walked into the room magnificent as ever and as usual stared at Hunter for a few moments before sniffing at the Doc who had frozen solid in his chair, not moving.

"Hi, girl – good to see you," Hunter said before she leapt onto the bottom of the bed, right on top of his bad foot.

Hunter yelped silently and pulled his bad foot away to let her scratch away at the bottom covers to make herself comfortable and then she glared at Jez and Doc as if protecting her human.

Doc started to say something and she stared straight at him. His lips refused to form any words of sense and he just carefully got up and left the room followed by a smiling Jez who shut the door.

"I thought the young human was going to say something that I would understand – why did he leave?"

"New friends, girl," Hunter murmured before she swung around to him and growled.

"Yea I know, I know, broken all the rules."

She turned back to find herself in the most comfortable place she had experienced in her life and stretched her legs before snuggling herself down, taking the bottom half of the bed but was interrupted in her comfort by a movement.

The door to the room began opening slowly – Hunter and the wolf became alert.

A large black head appeared.

"Sorry, mister, it's only me. I was just wondering about my dressing gown...oh my God, what is that?"

The wolf jumped down from the bed and went straight to Betty, sniffing her up and down.

"Another kind of human. I met one of you before – this one smells of hope!"

"Relax, ma'am, she's just saying hello – put your hand out and let her see you."

Betty put her hand out as the door opened fully and the wolf sniffed her all over, rubbing her head on her huge thighs.

"My...my, she is a friendly dog," Betty said looking down at Winter who stopped her greeting affections upon hearing the word dog.

"You are a dog ain't you?"

Her eyes narrowed before looking straight into Betty's eyes and growling lowly.

"Now what do you think, lady human?"

"Whatever she is, she is just beautiful," Betty replied.

"Dressing gowns hanging on the chair, Betty," Hunter advised as she picked up her garment and sniffed at it.

"Oh damn, now I'm' gonna smell like a wolf," Betty mumbled as she backed out of the room quietly shutting the door.

Winter then leapt back onto her comfortable bed, curled up and slept.

Hunter sat up for most of the night. Another bottle of whiskey was available but he ignored it, he was thinking.

The next morning came and Hunter had the plan in his mind. If they wanted him to kill a sniper, then he would. He had done it before, and he would do it again. Firstly, he needed eyes on Ma. He wanted to know what was happening in Gackle.

The wolf had wandered stealthily around the bar during the night as Hunter was awake planning and she had come back to the room satisfied that there was no danger here. She'd had some fun however with a drunk gay guy, who had fallen asleep behind one of the couches in the bar and had been missed by Jez when he'd shut the bar down. She laid herself alongside him and as he awoke from his drunken sleep, she raised her front left and hind leg over the man as if to give the human a cuddle and rubbed him with her paws before yawning and laying on her back stretching her legs up in the air.

"How was that for you, human?"

He froze in fear and she gave him a huge lick on his face before disappearing back into the dark.

***

"Do you guys have a bike that is not Harley Davidson and does not make a lot of noise?" Hunter asked Jez the next morning.

"OK yea, Steven has a Triumph Bonneville 750cc; it's a pretty English classic, full of chrome and piss – it looks fairly normal. I think I know what you mean."

"I need him to do one run past a house and observe, and I mean only observe, nothing else."

"Where is the house?"

"Gackle, North Dakota"

"Gackle? Do they breed geese there?"

"Jez, last time somebody said that there was a fist fight – let me talk to Steven. I need to brief him when he does this; it's important, then I want to go see where Phil was shot, and before we do this, can you guys get me some new clothes, something plain, I don't want no leather jacket!"

Doc smiled and went around the bikers' rooms searching for donations. None of them were as small as Hunter but he managed to rustle up a pair of jeans, matching jean jacket, t-shirt and sweater. His boots were the only things to survive Doc's assault with a pair of surgical scissors. He also found a brand-new pair of socks much to Hunter's delight.

"Junior, you make me feel like it's Christmas," Hunter said happily, gently easing the first sock over his bandaged foot. The pain in his chest and belly had returned slightly but he could manage this, he reckoned; he'd had enough morphine to last him a lifetime.

Hunter along with the wolf drove off for the first time in their new vehicle following Jez and the bikers to the area that Phil had been shot. It was on the other side of the town and as they drove through the main street, Hunter noticed the stares from the townsfolk before taking station a lot further back to disassociate himself with them. The wolf was in the back exploring their new vehicle; she now knew to keep hidden and Hunter had closed all the small curtains in the back of the RV.

They drove on for a couple of miles outside town until the landscape flattened out – nothing around but dirt and a few small rocks on the ground. Hunter caught up with the bikers as they pulled off the road and stopped. Hunter got out of the VW quickly followed by the wolf who sniffed the air before running off into the distance.

"Hey Hunter, I like your name, is it real?" Jez asked as Hunter limped towards them.

"Sure is dude, it was that or Geronimo; my Pa was a crazy man."

"You remind me of an Apache, are you sure we're not blood brothers from somewhere down the line?"

"Nah, I sometimes wished so, maybe it's because I grew up with them. I must have picked up some of their bad habits."

Hunter stopped the conversation by turning to observe the scene; he was in no mood for family talk.

Jez explained to him what had happened in detail and as Hunter listened, the biker finished with,

"So we reckon the shot came from somewhere over there."

Hunter followed his pointing arm and was not surprised at all at his next comment.

"Just about where your wolf is sitting."

They all made their way towards the wolf about 300 yards away from the main road.

As they reached her, she got up and began pawing at the ground.

Hunter looked down and noticed bike tracks going over the area, then he saw what he was looking for – a small piece of chord that shouldn't really be there. Pulling at it, he uncovered a shooting pit similar to what he'd found in Vietnam when he had been on that sniper hunt. The pit had been dug out to accommodate quite a large individual Hunter noticed. The ones back in Vietnam were a lot smaller for obvious reasons. She stood in the pit sniffing around before depositing a huge dump of scat in the middle of the shallow hole; this time it was pure American beef scat.

"You're one step ahead of me, girl. If I possessed a grenade then I would have rigged up a booby. I guess yours is just as potent."

"I've told you before, human, just ask me, and by the way, I have something else to show you when we get back to that awful place; can we go then?"

Hunter then really realised the seriousness of the situation; they couldn't leave just yet. He had probably been saved from a long painful death once again, by these people and felt indebted.

The bikers had remained silent watching proceedings. Jez did not have to call in any big guns, he had the biggest right next to him.

"Do you have any weapons, guys?"

"Not really," Jez answered quickly.

"Couple of shotguns and a few handguns, we ain't really that type of people; we just run a bit of hash for our money and then spend it enjoying ourselves. We're peace lovers – you might have noticed," Jez explained.

"You guys ain't really Hell's Angels, what are you?"

"Hunter we are an 'MC' – motorcycle club – we drive around on bikes and live life in the free – we don't ask this government for anything and we don't take anything from it – we look after places like Bettys and we make a living – we ain't One Percenters, we know them – and I could call them in right now but they would trash this town and we don't want that. You seem like a good option to help us out bro, wolf and all."

"What do you call yourselves?"

"Hey dude, we're the Nomads; we move around and we live nowhere, well, apart from Betty's."

Hunter thought for a little while – he needed friends and they were offering friendship.

"Well, I need you guys to help me get my friend out of North Dakota."

"Gackle, Hunter?" Jez asked.

"Sure thing, Jez. I hope Steve's done what I said; a good friend of mine is being held there by people looking for me and her," Hunter explained.

"That will be the FBI then," Doc suddenly interjected remembering Hunter's story.

Hunter didn't quite know if it was the FBI or some other organised company. He just knew what he knew. He gathered the bikers around him with a wave of his hands. "This is the deal boys – we, or I will kill the sniper, and you have to help me get my friend out from the place that she is at."

"Am I part of this plan?"

The bikers didn't hesitate; they all shook Hunters hand and thought about stroking the wolf before she got a bit agitated, then they left leaving Hunter to expertly put the shooting pit back into its untouched state.

"What was that strange ritual?"

"Girl, when you shake on a deal, the deal has to be done."

Hunter with the wolf drove cautiously back through the town. She knew now that she had to be hidden when other humans were around, apart from the ones that she had been formally introduced to and laid in the back of the VW quite enjoying the virgin smell of the new vehicle – no memories, just the smell of him and her.

At one stage, they stopped at a set of traffic lights and Hunter saw a large man on crutches shouting at three other men that were with him. Holding his hand up to cover his face, he took a memory photograph of the big guy's friends that included a high-ranking police officer. Hunter could tell this because of the uniform he was wearing, then the lights changed and he moved on.

They drove into the parking lot of 'Sweet Home Chicargo' and Hunter parked up close to the boundary, the furthest away from the bar he could get.

"Stay here, girl. I'll rustle up some grub and be back soon." Two nights in a bed was enough for Hunter, he needed a firmer surface to sleep on.

Just before he left the driver's side, she grabbed on to his new jean jacket and looked at him eyes moving at a frantic speed.

Hunter got it in an instant.

"You want to show me something," this was an answer, not a question.

He hobbled out of the VW looking around but it was all quiet.

She ran out of the cab over the boundary and into the long grass.

Hunter searched around following the boundary as it arched around the bar finding nothing until eventually, she called out to him, just a little wolf sound.

"Oh, come on, human – keep up with me."

He hobbled another 50 yards and found her laying on her back in the flattened grass, legs in the air.

She spotted him and got up, sniffing all around before sitting down the same, as she had done earlier that day, in a completely arrogant pose, informing Hunter that she had something important to tell him.

Hunter read the sign, big man, laid down, two indents in the flattened grass, elbow marks, spotter – shooter would have left one. It hadn't happened but it was possibly going to.

She then gave him another small bite to his arm and showed him the trail leading to the wooden copse outside of the parking lot area. Almost at the area she stopped and Hunter's nose got that familiar smell.

"Aw man, you are cruel; you left a Cajun chicken booby trap for him!"

Hunter noticed a hand print in the disgusting pile of Scat and giggled before moving around and following the wolf to the wooden copse next to the layby on the east side of the huge parking area. Hunter spotted the large tyre tracks in the dirt. An ATV.

"Thanks to you, girl, we don't have to go find him – he's coming here."

"I found him first, leave him to me."

"I'll deal with this from now on, girl – you've done enough."

They worked their way back to the sniper's firing point and Hunter looked up the large building in front of him picking out a particular window that would look down onto this position.

Hunter then picked up a broken stick and placed it on the bar side of the boundary mound, attaching a piece of white tissue paper that he found in the pocket of his new borrowed jeans.

Then they went back to the VW and slept for exactly two hours.

She could sleep all day and all night as long as she'd been fed; he only needed 2 hours out of 24.

Hunter woke and picked up the blanket covered M16A1 along with his rucksack full of ammo and of course, the Russian sights.

Walking into the bar, he caught the eye of Jez and they went upstairs. Counting the rooms, Hunter found the one he was looking for. Two bikers were smoking some weed before Hunter turned off the lights.

"Any of you guys fired an M16 before?"

They both shook their heads in silence.

"Hey, Hunter, what's happening?" Jez asked.

Hunter didn't answer, he was planning. Unrolling the blanket, they could just make out the M16 now laid on the bed. Hunter picked out the long Russian sights from the rucksack and opened the window looking down towards his target area.

He immediately picked out the stick with the white tissue and was satisfied.

"We ain't got to go find him, Jez, he's coming here," Hunter said confidently.

"Is this where you're gonna kill him from?"

Hunter ignored the question, he was still planning – if's, buts and more if's?

"I just need a constant watch on this position."

Hunter handed the sights to Jez who looked out amazed at what he could see close up.

"What am I looking for, Hunter?"

"See that little stick with the white marker on it, just straight out of here and to your right on the border verge, get it?"

Jez's untrained eye finally got it.

"Oh yea, who put that there?"

Hunter banged his own forehead with his hand.

"Me, you dumb arse! Just behind that small rise is where he's been observing from. I need one of your guys to keep watch; they won't see much, just a piece of grass moving – if he presents his weapon you will see it."

"What then, Hunter?"

"I'm still working on it," Hunter said thoughtfully.

Winter would want to help. Hunter knew that and he couldn't guarantee where she would be so with that in mind, he wrapped up Mickey's M16A1 and put it under one of the beds ordering nobody to touch it. Wolf ambush, now there was a thought.

The sound of loud Harleys returning to the bar filled the air. They were Phil's burial party; they had taken him on his last ride and buried him alongside the remains of their other two friends in a secret place with much respect. The authorities didn't need to know this and probably wouldn't care much anyhow. Just another dead biker.

***

Hunter had spent the best part of an hour with 'Steven', the rider of the 750cc Triumph Bonneville. Big as it was it didn't give off the unmistakable growl of a Harley, just a gentle purr really.

Stevens's father had also been in Vietnam and had died in a fire fight in 1970. His only big memory of his father was this machine.

His death had happened the day before that he had been due to come home. He'd suffered dreadfully for his loss, bullied at school, couldn't get even the most mediocre job and when he turned 18, he just jumped on this father's bike and rode out, eventually ending up at 'Sweet Home Chicargo' one year before, this was to become his new home.

Hunter drew him a diagram of Ma's road and told him where to drive in and where to drive out.

A half mile further down the road was an abandoned petrol station.

"What exactly do you want me to do?" the young man asked keen to help.

"There will be a vehicle parked outside of the property somewhere. I can't tell you exactly where; it will be left or right side of the road, the windows will not be blacked out and there will be people inside. Make sure you're gas is really low and tell them you're a bit lost and someone told you there was a gas station somewhere around there. Do you know anyone in North Dakota?"

"I had a girlfriend from up there once; she was from Bismarck, ain't too far away from Gackle."

"Perfect! She dumped you the night before and you're just trying to get home; you met with her in a bar – don't give any addresses away."

"Hey, how did you know that? That's exactly how it happened. I never knew where she lived."

Hunter smiled, sometimes, he surprised himself.

"Good man, I don't want you to do too much; just see what they look like, how they are dressed and how they sound."

"Nonchalant, Mister, that's what I'll be."

"Perfect description of how I want you to be – no dramatics kid."

"No drama, Hunter. I'll be as loose as a goose, after all I'm in Gackle, ain't I?"

"Yea cut that out funny guy; I got a punch in the mouth when I said those words!"

Steven smiled, he liked this little guy and was a little in awe but especially pleased that someone had finally taken him seriously and he really wanted to help. Hunter gave him a bundle of dollars and a good luck pat on his back.

***

Hunter walked into the bar and joined Jez and Doc. Big, black Betty was behind the counter and produced another huge steak wrapped in kitchen paper.

"That's for your Dog, mister or can I call you by your real name, Hunter, ain't it?"

"Sure is, ma'am," Hunter replied pulling another wad of dollars from his pocket and sliding it across the bar. He had never possessed so much cash before in his life and was enjoying himself, living the life and realising something about himself; he was actually a very kind person. Vicious to his enemies but kind to his friends.

Taking the money, she sang to him in Gospel, another tune that he and his comrades had sung together.

"You are a God send."

"God has sent me," Hunter replied,

"To do his bidding?"

"We praise the Lord, we don't praise ourselves," Hunter answered the singing prayer.

"In the dark of our despair we reach out and you are there. In the darkness," she sang quietly.

"In the darkness," he replied.

"In the darkness," she began to build the song.

"In the darkness," the final answer from Hunter sung badly but loud.

"In the darkness," she sang loudly and held the note before pausing at the end of her top 'C'

to look at hunter who was ready for the next line.

"We always know you care," they sang together.

They received a round of applause from Jez Doc and the rest of the bikers in the bar.

"Hunter, can I buy you a drink?" Betty asked.

Hunter smiled wryly before answering.

"Give me a bottle of pussy water, please Betty," the local term for mineral water.

The bikers didn't remark, they were grateful to have a professional killer on their side.

"Hunter, you need to have a bath soon. I need to change your dressings," Doc said to him.

"Later, Junior," Hunter replied – he was on another mission and didn't have time for small things.

"Hey Betty, do you have any events coming up soon?"

Hunter thought that the sniper would want to have a big impact when he killed this time, according to the research he was putting in.

"Not really Hunter, we just the same most nights but there is a gay march going on in Minnesota City this Saturday, so I can imagine that a lot of the guys will come here after to party out."

That was all Hunter needed to know, it would be this weekend. Oh, how he wished he had a couple of grenades that he could set booby's from; there was a whole box of them in Mickey's store but he had just chosen the big beast mine.

He had so enjoyed setting the claymore, in between the legs of the Chippewa Indian after what they had done to him. He had used a whole role of sellotape to bind the Indian and setting the charge, wondering if the thing would even go off but as he had closed the door to the ATV with the arming wire attached to the door handle, he was sure that he had heard the comforting pre-armed click of the device. One more pull on the wire would give a two-second warning before the explosion. The Indian behind the mine died because of the blast bursting his lungs; the ones in front of it were hit by a cocktail of ball bearings and sharp metal objects.

Hunter spent the next couple of days preparing, mostly in his killing room; he had swapped rooms with the two bikers and had taken two tall stools from the bar to fashion into a shooting platform from where he could sit comfortably for as long as it took. One of the panes of glass had been removed from the window which would give him a clear shot down onto his target area and just look like a closed window in the dark. He completely stripped-down Mickey's precious weapon and meticulously cleaned it within an inch of its life before reassembling it, checking every component. He also practiced removing and reattaching the huge Russian sights with the four butterfly nuts getting the difficult procedure down to 16 seconds. He checked every round in the three full magazines, sitting on the bed and lovingly cleaning the ordinance.

Unfortunately, he would not be able to range the gun in; that would give too much away but he was sure he could work out the correct angle required knowing that it shot high.

Although the two bikers had been moved out of the room, Hunter still insisted that they carry on the observation every evening.

His wounds were beginning to sour again and he had eventually succumbed to Doc's order and had a bath. After a painful session in hot salted water, Doc had redressed his bandages and given him yet another painful penicillin jab in his butt cheek.

"Ah man, are you sure you ain't part Indian yourself, junior?" Hunter had protested.

"You are not out of the woods just yet Hunter – just keep up the hygiene and you should be fine."

Doc smiled at the fact that this man's ability to deal with pain ended with a simple jab to his butt.

Winter had kept herself hidden from everyone, mostly sleeping on one of the bunks in the VW. Hunter had closed all the small window curtains and slept on the hard floor. Every so often she would go on her night patrols, standing all over Hunter before letting herself out and shutting the door behind. Not that he minded too much, he was awake most of the time.

"Just let me know when you're going out, girl – I'll move."

"You should know when I'm going out, human."

She was happy with her regular reconnoitre until the day came – Saturday. Just after the darkness had set in over the bar she slipped out for a final look around. On the opposite side of the parking lot from where she had found the first tracks, she found a new source, a new smell; different but the same.

She smelled another human – a human with a gun.

Winter hurried back to the VW and found Hunter waiting at the door for her. As she leapt onto the passenger seat, he quickly placed yet another huge steak provided by Betty on the seat, then proceeded to lock the door, quickly moving around to the driver's side to lock that one as well.

"Sorry, girl, there's gonna be gunfire. I don't want you out side when it goes off."

She frantically pawed at the windows but couldn't release the doors, she felt trapped.

"Stupid human, there's something else I have to show you!"

Hunter moved back into the bar to the darkened room and relieved the ever-attentive biker of Mickey's sights before reattaching them to the M16A1. He had practiced this manoeuvre a few times before thinking about the reason why the thing shot high; it was probably because Mickey had drilled the attachment holes into the side of the M16, just the tiniest of measurements out. It shot straight though and that's all Hunter needed.

"Bit of movement down there, just like you said it would be."

Hunter didn't answer – he was in kill mode; that little moment before the occurrence when all he could hear in his head was white noise cutting out the world, concentrating on the job in hand.

Hunter made himself comfortable in his shooting position and for the first time, spotted a movement in the target area.

Game on, cat and mouse mixed with chicken.

It was a full two hours before anything happened.

Scores of gay people had arrived and were gathered outside, slowly making their way into the bar being greeted by Betty, Jez and another couple of big bikers were at hand looking for anyone that shouldn't be there.

Hunter had briefed them all and had some vehicles parked in between the sniper's position and the entrance to the bar – even so, it wasn't completely safe.

A flicker of movement caught his eye; two dark circles of a large pair of binoculars taking one final look at their target. He tried to recognise the face behind them as they lowered but it was all camouflaged black with streaks of green and brown.

He remembered seeing two snipers coloured up and ready for their mission back in Vietnam. One would observe and the other would make the shot; both were capable of either. *Two big guys*, Hunter thought, *I wonder?* thinking about the flattened grass and the size of the shooting pit.

Hunter began to calm himself; breath slowly, reduce your heartbeat – no distractions, just the job in hand. He had the cross hairs of Mickey's weapon bang on, just below the rise of the border. Shoot low, shoot low – then out it came. A small cylindrical shape protruding – the weapon's silencer.

Hunter still waited playing chicken; the object moved left slightly, then right and then stopped. Target acquired. Hunter was just a split second ahead of him.

He let loose three quick accurate rounds before switching the gun to fully automatic and emptying the full magazine into the area.

He quickly attached a fresh magazine and waited. In the garbled white noise in his mind, there was silence.

Then the 'zing' sound of a bullet passed under his window heading for the entrance to the bar.

"Damn! There's two of them and they've got a crossfire!" he shouted cursing himself.

Downstairs in the bar, pandemonium occurred. Everyone had run for cover as Hunter had emptied the magazine of his

M16 but there were still a lot of people outside the safety of the bar.

Betty at the entrance had felt the bullet entering and exiting her huge thigh before collapsing to the floor, pleading silently with her eyes to Doc and Jez who were safe and just a matter of inches away from her.

"HEY, THEY GOT BETTY!" Hunter heard as he hobbled as quickly as he could downstairs to the bar carrying his weapon.

Hunter reached the main door – Jez and Doc were looking at Betty prone on the floor bleeding heavily from her wound.

Two of Jez's friends and three or four gay guys were also down but obviously dead. Silence then reigned once again. Hunter knew that the killer was using her as bait, the way the Viet Cong worked.

"What do we do now, Hunter?" the young Doc asked in desperation wanting to get to Betty as soon as possible.

Hunter took one look at the situation and just walked out, staring at where the shot would have come from holding Mickey's M16A1 lowly, standing in front of the prone Betty moaning at the pain from her wound.

"Breath, Betty. If you are breathing then you are still alive," Hunter advised.

"I'm still breathing, Hunter."

"I might not be soon, Betty."

"Trust her, Hunter," he thought he heard Betty shout to him.

White noise surrounded his ears like a boxer in a ring as he waited for the inevitable. One again he was the bait!, but this time he felt more like a lamb being led to slaughter –

Hunter couldn't help himself, he felt that it was the right thing to do.

The other sniper looked through his sights and mumbled angrily to himself, "I'll be damned – that's Hunter Wisekat with Tomlin's sights, the PSO1; they should have been mine and all you idiots could do was glue them onto a God damned useless M16A1... Oh, well you skinny little rat, I'll see you in hell!"

Just before he pulled the trigger, his blood froze as he sensed danger from behind and his whole life suddenly flashed before his eyes.

Taking the slightest look from the corner of his left eye, the last thing he ever saw was a dark figure flying through the air that he understood to be the grim reaper coming to take him home.

Her lower jaw caught his windpipe and the other clamped down onto the back of his neck. Her body then twisted still in mid-flight and her heavy weight broke his neck, almost tearing his head away from the body.

Only then did she make the sound of a monster beast ripping into her prey.

At the bar they heard her ripping the man apart and Doc ran to Betty's aid. She had taken a shot to her ample thigh but it wasn't life-threatening and he managed to stem the flow of blood quickly.

Hunter ran/hobbled to the first sniper's position and blasted the body with a short burst to make absolutely sure before carrying on to the second.

Winter trotted towards him triumphantly, blood dripping from her jaws but he just ran past her. He had to know the sniper was dead and not just wounded. He reached the point and found the remains of the man still holding his weapon. His head had almost been decapitated and was at a perverse angle to his body.

Hunter recognised the face even though it was coloured in black, green and brown stripes.

"Oh hi, Richard! I expect that's the other Richard over there – man; you were always a pair of dicks."

Hunter spoke to the dead mutilated body and picked up his weapon and three spare magazines of ten-round ammunition that were in close reach of the sniper. Hunter knew that he and the wolf had stopped an absolute bloodbath.

"Oh man this is the ugliest gun in the world, just like you – you bucket head." Hunter spoke to the dead body with excitement; he knew what it was but needed a closer look to make sure.

Richard and Richard were a famous sniper team back in the day. They were both a pair of psychopaths who enjoyed their work and were always destined to do their business commercially after they had left the army. They didn't even like each other but worked so well together.

On this occasion, Richard1 had reluctantly called in his old partner to help him with this shoot – he would have to share the bounty money. He hadn't told him however that he had been stalked by a wolf when observing, and it wasn't a complete 'turkey shoot' of bikers and gays, the description he had used when he had sold the job to him.

Back in Vietnam, Hunter's team had been given the mission to take out a serious Viet Cong sniper at the time Richard & Richard had been granted some RNR. When they saw the long Russian sights that Mickey had proudly displayed to them on their return to the camp, they hadn't been exactly pleased.

Hunter walked back towards the bar but was immediately confronted by a now angry wolf.

"How many times do I have to tell you, human – leave it to me!"

"I couldn't leave this one to you, girl – too many bullets, that's why I locked you away; how'd you get out anyhow?"

"Hadn't you noticed that our new home has four doors; you only locked two."

"Yea, yea, I knew that you would find the other way out. In fact, I was relying on it," Hunter lied.

Hunter stopped at the sound of sirens in the distance.

"We'll take a little walk away from here, girl – just until the dust settles eh?"

Hunter went back to the first position and picked up the sniper's weapon and two more magazines. Hunter recognised him even though his face had been obliterated; he also knew the weapon, a standard McMillan Tac-338. Putting all the spare magazines into a canvas bag that Richard1 had by his side, he beckoned the wolf to follow him.

With that they walked into the long grass, putting distance between themselves and the bar. Hunter carried the three rifles and found a slight rise where they could sit and observe. They watched as many emergency vehicles with the blue flashing lights came and went, the first one hopefully transporting Betty to the local hospital. Later, Hunter found out that the chief of police from the town had visited and had personally ordered the removal of the bodies of three gay guys and the two snipers. Jez had hidden the bodies of his two fallen men for a respectful burial in their personal space. This chief of police hadn't asked much – after all he had contributed some of the town's finances to the hiring of the sniper.

Hunter and Winter sat together for a while, him humming that Marcus Malone song.

"Well, I heard it through the grapevine that you're big bad wolf is coming home."

"And your little red riding hood, is gonna know that you've been up to no good."

"But these comp' comp' complications, are killing me."

They sat together for a while watching the blue flashing lights and listening to the sirens coming and going until Hunter thought it was safe to move.

"Our work is done here, girl," Hunter said gently to Winter.

"Oh good, can we go now?"

"We can't leave just yet though; need to sort out the other half of the deal. We have to save Ma."

The wolf's ears pricked up at the word Ma and they looked at each other silently in the dark.

"Leave that to me, human."

"I can't leave that to you, girl – we have to be a good team for my plan to work out – are you OK with that?"

"Whatever you say, human. Let's just get out of here – it's awful."

Hunter then fussed around the rifle taken from Richard2; even in the dark he could make out that this was not an American weapon – Russian, "*I wonder*," he thought to himself detaching the sights from Mickeys M16A1 using the quick release butterfly nuts. He rummaged around the canvas bag taken from Richard1 and found a Swiss army knife. Selecting a flat head screwdriver, he took off the small sights from the Russian gun. He then attached the long Dragunov sights to the weapon that they finally belonged to. The gun was also Dragunov. They went together like a new married couple, perfect for each other as long as you kept the relationship clean and aligned with each other, now and then.

The ones he took off were also Dragunov but a smaller 'SVD Ohhunt' version. He carried on watching proceedings through the POS1 sights.

"Oh man you are ugly, but you are one hell of a killing machine."

Hunter spoke to the gun...

"I do hope you are not referring to me, human?"

Hunter mused, knowing that this weapon in the right hands could kill from almost two miles away. And now they were in the right hands.

Hunter then took out the three American magazines to leave with the McMillan but also picked out a white envelope containing yet another huge wad of dollars – the bounty money for killing the bikers.

"This is one hell of a way to get rich, girl," Hunter murmured.

"Rich? I feel like the poorest being in the world, human."

Hunter still needed Mickey's bastardised M16A1 for short range assault purposes, so he just left the American rifle and the small Russian sights along with the ammo. He always needed to travel light. Maybe someone would find them one day in this abandoned field; maybe he would come back for them, he didn't know. Giving the weapon a respectful pat, they got up and made their way back to the bar. Hunter knew that the word would get around about a wolf being in the area and they had to get out of there sooner than later.

He hid the weapons under one of the bunks in the RV and Winter settled down on the other looking at him.

Noticing the side door had been opened, he smiled at her before closing it up on his way out of the VW.

Once again, she had saved his life.

"Won't be long, girl," he spoke gently before he headed to the bar.

She licked the rest of the human blood from around her jaws and also found the steak that Hunter had earlier left for her.

In her frantic state, she had nearly bitten through the door handles trying to get out before calming herself and trying to think like a human. She had gone to the back of the RV and after a lot of thought and sniffing around, she cleverly worked out the mechanism for the side sliding door. After getting outside, she had positioned herself in the middle of the two snipers' firing points and waited, not knowing which one to kill, but as Hunter had obliterated the first, she had run headlong to the second.

She ate her reward and laid on her bunk impatiently. "Can we go now?"

Entering the bar, Hunter walked past six bikers who were guarding the front door; they each gave him a respectful pat on his back and shoulders as he walked past them not wanting to be too obvious in their appreciation.

"Ooh man, I finally got a guard of honour." he mused silently.

Spotting Jez and Doc, he pointed upwards and at the same time made the drink signal with his right hand.

Oh yes, Hunter needed a drink. The bar was full of crying, hysterical gay guys and as he walked up the stairs, Doc followed leaving Jez to get a bottle.

Hunter then pointed to his bum cheek and Doc smiled – this man has a serious humour problem.

"You do realise that alcohol reduces the potency of penicillin Hunter!" Doc advised as they went into the nearest private room.

"Yea, yea, yea, yea!" Hunter replied, settling himself down on the comfortable bed before immediately getting up and dropping his pants. Bending over and offering his bum cheek toward the Doc who took out another long needle full of penicillin from his leather doctors' case and jabbed it into Hunters rear end, squeezing the contents out and making Hunter moan painfully.

"I'm sorry, am I disturbing something here?" Jez said playfully as he walked in with a fresh bottle of whiskey and three glasses.

Hunter pulled up his pants and sat down gently on the edge of the comfortable bed before getting down to business.

He lit a cigarette and downed a large whiskey before breathing heavily trying to remove the white noise from his brain, the same way he had done after every mission.

"You OK, Hunter?" they both said, concerned as they watched something similar to 'Dr Jekyll becoming Mr Hyde' once again.

Finally, Hunter gained his composure, opened his eyes and looked down to the floor to announce happily.

"Hey guys, I didn't 'sick up – ain't you the lucky ones?"

Hunter was only joking but now they took anything he said very seriously.

"Did Steven call in?" Hunter asked already planning for the second mission, lighting up another cigarette that Jez had offered.

"On his way back now, Hunter; says he has something interesting to tell you. He should be here early tomorrow morning," Jez answered.

"Then we have to leave guys; there are some serious people after my girl and we need somewhere else to hang out before we go get my friend – any ideas?"

"What do you know about the Yankton Sioux Hunter?" Jez asked.

"Apart from the fact that I know that you're part of one of them, and I have killed some of your enemies, oh yea and one of your old chiefs was called 'Chief Butt Face' or something – not a lot."

Hunter replied immediately regretting his disrespectful answer.

"That was 'Chief Smutty Bear'," Jez corrected him somewhat angrily.

"Oh yea, I'm sorry, man – his name was 'MA-TO-SA-BE-CHE-A' to be precise."

Hunter surprised Jez with the revered chief's Indian name, rescuing the situation and surprising Jez once again at his wealth of knowledge of Indian history.

"Well, you can go stay with my cousin Ken in South Dakota on the reservation if that's OK with you two; being Apache scum that you obviously are, you will be allowed."

Jez advised still annoyed at Hunter's comment about their revered chief; only bona fide Native American Indians were allowed to venture into reservations.

"Can I call myself Geronimo?" Hunter asked.

"No, Hunter, you will be called 'little skinny bitch man with a wolf'. That is your password onto the reservation. I'll tell him you're coming."

Jez answered before bursting into uncontrollable laughter.

Hunter knew that this was true; without a password or a proper Indian name, he would not be allowed in.

"Tell me that in Sioux language, you damned beefcake," Hunter requested knowing that Jez was laughing to take away the horrors of the past few hours.

Jez suddenly sobered and looked at Hunter affectionately and offered his hand to him.

"Thanks man, I'll write it down for you tomorrow," the big guy said before bursting into tears.

Hunter patted him on the back affectionately as he left the room.

"Yea man, I know where you're at. Let the river flow and smile when you reach your destination."

Hunter made his way from the bar and settled down inside the VW on the hard floor. She didn't even wake up when he came in – even in sleep she knew it was him.

***

The gentle purr of a Triumph Bonneville 750cc filled Hunter's ears early the next morning. Steven was back.

The whole area was quiet so he indicated to Winter to come into the bar with him.

Steven's face said everything as he got off the bike to be greeted with Hunter and a huge wolf at his side.

"Oh man, is that her?" Steven asked as he looked into her ever-staring eyes, again being hypnotised by her look and maybe thoughts. She blinked and only then could he move or say anything.

"She is beautiful," Steven could only utter.

The doors to the bar open and Jez ushered the three of them in to the smell of fresh coffee.

They sat downstairs in the bar for their meeting – the whole of Jez's MC club was there…

Winter got it first; she was all over Steven, sniffing and yelping excitedly as soon as he sat down in a large armchair.

"He smells of care!"

Hunter got it straight away.

"Hey Steven, you met my Ma, didn't you?"

"Is that old lady your Ma? I thought your name was Hunter. She just kept calling me Mickey."

"Yea, Mickey was a good friend of mine; he was her son. How did you get into the house, I told you not to do too much?" Hunter asked worriedly.

"I couldn't help it Hunter, it was just a chain of events," Steven replied thinking that he'd done the wrong thing.

"I did exactly as you said; the car was on the left side of the road and I pulled alongside the guy on the passenger side and asked him about the gas station which he didn't know. The other guy came out of the car and told me that the place had been abandoned for a year. Then he stared messing with my bike. I think he kinda liked it and the first thing that he looked for was the gas gauge just like you said they would. He asked me where I'd been, where I was going and at the same time the other guy was talking into a microphone checking me out, I suppose. Then, the second guy said to me that he'd really love to drive my bike for a little while and they would give me some gas. I said well fine, mister you can do that but I am desperate for the bathroom, is there somewhere here I can go?

"Then..." Steven paused to take a deep breath.

"The guy who liked my ride spoke to the one on the C/B who made another call. Then after a couple of minutes one of the gates opened and I was invited in."

"What clothes were they wearing?" Hunter asked.

"I thought about that Hunter, about what you had said and it was quite strange; the one who got on my bike was all casual but the one in the driver's seat was wearing a suit as was the one who took me into the house."

"That would have been a long walk, Steven," Hunter said knowing the distance between the gate and the house.

"Hunter that was the longest walk of my life squeezing my butt checks together, I really had to go."

"What did you hear then?" Hunter asked.

"All I heard was an old lady sound shouting, 'Mickey, is that you Mickey?' then I walked up a few steps to the house and another guy wearing a suit guided me into the toilet next to the kitchen; do you know where I am Hunter?"

"Oh yea."

"Well, I did number ones, numbers two's and even number three's and when I got out of the can, the old lady just jumped on me shouting, Mickey, Mickey!"

Hunter knew what Ma had done; she had laid her scent for Winter, that's why she had fussed all over him.

"Yea man, then two guys grabbed her off me and took her away, telling me she had lost her mind and she wanted to kill the President, so they were looking after her."

Hunter almost went into a kill politician mode before controlling himself.

So far Hunter had counted eight men in attendance, two at the gates, two inside with Ma. There would be another two dealing with communications and another two at the back of the building lying in wait, plus two for good measure and he also guessed that they would be bored out of their tiny minds at this project. Nothing much had happened until Steven arrived and they had checked him out from top to bottom. He was clear.

"Oh yea, Hunter – you know what the strangest thing was?" Steven said.

"Go Guy!"

"Man, they were all old, I mean you are old to me, but these guys were really old, grey hair or no hair at all, and I mean all of them. The one who drove my bike looked even older than my dad but he reminded me of how my dad would have been if he was still alive – still loving the bike."

"Yea, man, I understand."

"Then I made my apologies for leaving a dump smell in their house and they let me go."

Hunter got up and embraced the young man which was probably the first time in his life that he had ever shown any type of affection for another male in all of his life, Mickey was different, they just used to punch each other.

"Oh man, God does love a volunteer," Hunter said as he squeezed the young man.

"I want to hug him too, he smells of care!" Winter thought as she joined in a three-way hug letting out a huge, "*AWoooooooooo,*" to which the bikers in the bar all followed, "*AWooooooo.*"

They all joined in the gang hug and sang, which made Winter feel that she was finally back in a pack for the first time since she'd left Canada.

When the wolf pack singing died down, Hunter's suspicious mind then kicked in once again.

"Hey Steven, let me see your bike," he ordered and everyone went silent.

They all followed Hunter as he hobbled out of the bar towards Steven's Triumph.

Winter sniffed around the bike and began growling softly at a particular area.

Hunter searched around the area feeling with his hands and eventually pulled out a device from underneath the petrol tank, held on with magnets that was still flashing little white lights.

Hunter held the thing and looked at the bikers before shrugging his shoulders. They had all seen this in James Bond movies but now it was right in front of them.

Hunter took the device back into the bar and ordered another coffee. Placing the device on a table he stared at it for the next hour. "If? What if? And if? And why?"

He knew that it was a pretty crude device and for it to work, they would have had to follow Steven with a tracking team based in some large vehicle; it was only a short-range device maybe 20 miles at the best. Hunter guessed that they might have followed Steven for a while to make sure he was not meeting up with anyone close by and then given up the chase as he drove through North Dakota into Minnesota. Maybe there was a mobile team out there somewhere trying to find the signal but he doubted it. However, if there was even a sniff of a wolf being in Minnesota, then the triangulation would put them straight at their doorstep.

"Get me some lead, Jez!" Hunter ordered suddenly coming into action.

"How much do you need, Hunter?" Jez answered a little confused.

"Enough to cover this little box of tricks. I think we can use it later on."

Jez apologised to Betty in her absence before ordering a couple of his guys to get a ladder and strip off a small length of lead from the roof.

Hunter bent the lead flashing around the small device and handed it to Jez.

"What happens with this, Hunter?" Jez asked suspiciously.

"We are going to need a diversion, Jez. You give this little baby to your One Percenter friends. We're going to need them."

"What can I say we'll give them in return, Hunter?"

"Weapons, Jez – lots of them."

"I think they'll go along with that."

Hunter offered Jez another roll of dollars but the big guy declined.

"No Man, you've saved all our lives, least we can do is help you out."

Winter growled lowly looking at Jez who now realised that this wolf was really something special.

"Oh, I'm sorry, honey! How could I forget about you; can I give you a rub?"

"No, you cannot."

Just as they were leaving, Jez handed Hunter a small deerskin headband with his tribe's inscription,

"Wear this, Hunter, you'll be OK."

Hunter knew the significance of this item; it was Jez's own and it carried the sign of peace.

"Thank you, my brother – maybe we are related after all."

With that, Hunter and Winter departed. Jez had given him directions for the Yankton Sioux reservation and instructions for what to do when he got there. Five minutes later, they were heading for South Dakota.

***

The big man on crutches limped into the mortuary and stood alongside the, chief of police, looking at the grizzled remains of Richard2 whose neck had been broken and his face severely mutilated.

He looked over to the other body whose face and torso had been completely obliterated by gunfire.

"Oh My God – what the hell happened, chief?"

"Well, as far as I can work out, one was shot several times and the other has been mutilated by a wild animal," the chief of police stated the obvious, already bored by this arrogant man's attitude...

The big guy fussed around for a little while before asking.

"What kind of animal?"

"Well, it wouldn't have been a T-rex, that would have bit him in half, maybe a smaller creature like a velociraptor, but in this day and age no, it was probably something like a cheetah or lion or maybe even a wolf!" The chief of police said sarcastically.

The big arrogant man became aloof.

"Can we keep this under our hats for a little while, chief? We have a nice town here and I want to keep it that way."

"Whatever you say, Frank, you are the head of the council," the chief of police replied.

"If it was a wolf, then it would have been that wolf and I have some friends who are looking for it," the big hunk replied.

"Oh that wolf; didn't we have a bounty offered?" the chief of police surmised, realising that he was sending this complete and utter idiot into madness.

The big guy's face turned to thunder and he couldn't speak.

"That wolf was here and we missed out on twenty grand. It cost us three grand to hire the sniper man to take out the bikers and the gays but all the time the big prize was right here, and we missed it because of your dislike for people who don't tow your line, so what did your friends say, Frank? Who were we supposed to have been looking for in connection with the wolf?"

The big man squirmed visibly remembering his encounter with Hunter.

"A little skinny guy," was all he could say.

***

Hunter drove through the gates of the Yankton Sioux reservation and was stopped straight away by couple of men on horses riding bare back. They were obviously Native American Indians who both carried vintage, Winchester-style rifles that were now levelled at Hunter.

He had been wearing his new deerskin headband since he left Minnesota.

Winter had sniffed and licked at it wanting to eat it, before Hunter pushed her away, numerous times.

"Hey, girl – you seem to think my headdress is like a packet of chips donncha? You want it, but you can't have it!"

"I like it, and I will have it."

"No – you will not!"

"You ain't allowed here, mister," one of them ordered.

Hunter realised that the headband he was wearing wasn't enough to let him through.

"I've come to visit my cousin, he lives here."

The two Indians smiled at each other before carrying on their interrogation.

"So how does an Apache have a Sioux cousin?" one of them asked.

Hunter thought for a while before answering; they had mentioned Apache, so they must know who he was.

"Geronimo got about a bit, guys."

Probably the wrong answer as they became aggressive and road around the VW kicking up dust and whooping a war chant still pointing the Winchesters at him.

Both of them stopped on either side of the VW windows.

"And you are?" one of them questioned.

Hunter took a deep breath and reluctantly announced his new Indian name in perfect Sioux that Jez had written out for him and he had practiced on the drive to the reservation.

"Little skinny bitch man with a wolf."

The Indians steadied their horses and asked seriously.

"So where is your wolf, mister?"

Winter then showed herself alongside Hunter and looked left, then right at the Indians, holding each of their gazes for a second.

"I suppose you mean 'me', young humans?"

With that, the Indians beckoned Hunter to follow them and they rode deep into the reservation.

Hunter drove on for one more hour following the Indians on horseback, not now having to follow the sparse map that Jez had painted for him, getting stares from the Indians that he passed on the way; not knowing who he was and not believing their eyes as they recognised a real wolf alongside him. Eventually, they stopped at the top of a hill that looked down on a huge lake of water with a forest of green trees behind. Hunter's instant thought was for Ma, this was her dream place. There was a small group of houses built alongside the lake to which one of the Indians pointed to with his Winchester before they both left singing once again the woop call of Indians at war.

Hunter drove slowly to the houses and Winter gazed at the beautiful sight.

"Is this our new home? It's wonderful!"

Hunter arrived and stopped a few yards away from the first house.

In front of him, stood a huge Indian that reminded him of Jez, alongside an also large but old, husky dog.

Hunter worried for a while and as he opened the door to get out. Winter jumped across him and went straight for the dog and Indian who remained passive.

She ran around them sniffing and growling happily.

The old dog watched her and visibly shook in fear getting closer to his master's legs for protection before Winter sat and stared at him.

"Friends, girl – these are friends," Hunter advised.

"What a strange and beautiful world I'm in."

Hunter walked towards the Indian and made the peace sign with his right hand.

The Indian shrugged his shoulders and replied to Hunter in the same way before announcing.

"Yea man, that's sweet, but these days we just normally shake hands – you must be Hunter," the large Indian said offering his hand out.

"No man, I'm little bitch fella with a wolf – you must be Ken."

They shook a firm handshake observed by Winter.

"That ritual once again?"

With that, Ken's old, husky dog barked a small order to Winter before turning around and trotting into the forest surrounding the houses and lake.

"Don't worry Hunter, I think old Burt just wants to show her around. We think he is part wolf himself, so they'll be OK."

Winter for the first time looked at Hunter for guidance.

"Yea go on, girl, make yourself at home."

"Is this my new home? I do hope so!"

As the old Husky dog and Winter disappeared into the nearby forest, Ken's family appeared from the nearby houses.

"We saw her dad! Isn't she a wolf? Can we touch her when she comes back?"

A dozen kids arrived by Ken's side all jumping over him excitedly before all running off again as if they were a pack.

"Are they all your kids, Ken?" Hunter asked.

"I'm not really sure, I expect some of them are," Ken answered with a wicked smile on his face.

Hunter liked this guy's sense of humour.

"Come on into the house, you must be hungry."

Hunter walked with Ken into the house and they sat down at a huge kitchen table.

"Hi Hunter, I'm Nancy. Ken told me what you'd done for Jez; we are honoured to have you stay with us for a while," the woman standing and cooking at the huge stove said as they sat.

"Ma'am, the honour is all mine and the pleasure is gonna be all mine judging by what I can smell in that pot – you are cooking chilli."

"Sure am, Hunter; we thought a Southern boy like you would like a bit of home food – hope you don't mind the Indian twist I put in it, just a couple of deer testicles in there and the crunchy bits will be cow hoof shavings. They can get stuck in your teeth so I'm just warning you."

Hunter looked towards Ken who could not disguise his smile.

"Oh man, you two have the same sick sense of humour! How does that happen?"

Ken and his wife Nancy burst out laughing.

"Are you married, Hunter?" Ken asked, still giggling.

"I was once," Hunter lied putting on a sad face.

"What happened, Hunter?" Nancy asked looking serious.

Hunter made up the story in a second.

"Me and her were climbing up to a Plato back in Arizona, trying to find a secret water source and she slipped and fell dragging me down with her. I broke both my ankles but she hit her head and died straight away."

Hunter waited until they were hooked into the story.

"So what happened then?" Nancy asked concerned.

"Well, then I struggled to get to her knowing that we wouldn't be found for weeks by the authorities and then a huge bald eagle swooped down and began pecking at her face, so I picked up a rock and killed the son of a bitch with one throw."

"So how did it end, Hunter?" Ken asked starting to get where Hunter was coming from.

"Well, I survived for the next three weeks on wife meat and eagle meat. Oh man, that old bird was pretty tough, but the eagle meat tasted really good!"

Hunter's face lit up as he said the punch line.

"Nancy, he is one of us! Let me get this man a drink!"

Ken produced a large jug of homemade hooch and poured out three glasses before Nancy joined them at the table. Hunter then decided to indulge himself in a bit of RNR; he had earnt this privilege and began feeling totally at home with these two complete nut cases.

"So you've never even had a girlfriend I take it, Hunter?" Nancy enquired.

Hunter had experienced this third degree interrogation with Ma and went through his whole repertoire of answers.

"I've met lots of girls who were my friend but I've never had a girl that was my girlfriend; why's that Nancy? Do you have any attractive sisters or cousins about my age?"

"As a matter of fact, I do."

Hunter was only joking and Ken sensed him squirming' in his seat and changed the subject.

"Hunter, you get wasted tonight and relax for a while; from what Jez told me you need it – you're also still pretty sick man, I can see it in your face."

"Think I need some 'Indian healing, Ken," Hunter answered quietly.

Ken answered by refilling Hunter's glass as Nancy put down a huge bowl of chilli in front of him.

"Man, I have just died and gone to heaven," Hunter announced, greedily eating the spiced minced beef dish feeling the most relaxed he had been in a very long time.

The three of them sat drinking for the next few hours telling stupid jokes and wild stories to each other. Every now and then, members of Ken's family would come in to say hello and share a glass of his wicked brew. Finally, to ease Hunter's worries, the wolf arrived back greeted by screams of excitement from the children playing outside. Winter and Burt walked in, each triumphantly carrying a dead rabbit in their jaws. Nancy fussed over them like a proud mother and Winter even allowed her to rub her affectionately.

As usual Winter stared into Hunter's face for a while, causing a quiet hush as Ken and Nancy watched on.

"If you tell me we have to leave this place, human, I will kill you."

"I see you have a new hunting partner, girl – is he friendly?"

"You mean the dog wolf? He is bearable, he is kind and he is knowledgeable in the ways of a wolf, but we are in your world and he is not you."

The spiritual conversation was cut short as Ken produced a bowl of raw meat from the refrigerator and placed it on the floor. Burt attacked the meat greedily as Winter sat and watched him. After two mouthfuls, he suddenly paused and looked up at the wolf. Either he was being a gentleman or perhaps he was slightly scared; he backed off and allowed Winter to finish the bowl before they both went outside to be with the children. There were screams of delight as Winter allowed herself to be touched by the young humans.

Ken looked at his wife.

"You OK, babe?"

Nancy had just watched the proceedings silently in a semi-trance-like state and suddenly awoke – this action was not missed by Hunter.

"She speaks to you Hunter; I felt everything she was saying. Do you get that too?"

Hunter had not thought too much about it. He knew they had some sort of bond together through life and death and he had defiantly heard her calling to him in his mind as he walked into Richard2's crosshairs.

"More or less; sometimes her language is pretty bad. I couldn't repeat some of the things she's said to me in front of a lady. I think I need to wash her mouth out with soap sometimes."

Nancy frowned at him knowing he was joking 'badly'.

Ken smiled knowingly; this was one special wolf guy and they were indeed going to give him some 'special' Indian healing. He made a small excuse for leaving and made his way around to the back of the houses knowing that Nancy would keep him occupied for the next half hour – she could talk for the whole Indian nation.

In a huge tepee at the back of the house, Ken met with two of Nancy's sisters – twins.

"How are we doing, girls?" Ken asked unflinchingly; they were both naked from the waist up.

One of them checked out the hot coals in the fire and tested them with a cup of herb-fuelled water.

Steam gently arose from the hot rocks and the other replied.

"Not yet, Ken; give us another half hour – has he had the pill yet?"

"We're waiting for him to visit the John, so we can 'Mickey Finney' his drink; he hasn't gone since he's been here. Jez told me he's some hard, little man so you'd better be on your guard, girls – shout me if you need me. I won't be far away."

"Just bring him in, Ken – we'll take it from there."

"He's going to die and then be reborn?"

The girls ignored him and fussed around their healing items, lots of fresh spruce and a pot of herb-infused clay amongst other things.

Niki and Rebecca were Nancy's younger twin sisters who were the Yankton Sioux's foremost experts in the art of Indian healing. They were indeed the same age as Hunter but had he known what he was about to endure within the next twelve hours, then romance would be completely out of the question.

Ken walked back into the kitchen and heard Hunter relieving himself in the toilet in the downstairs' out room. Nancy winked at him.

Hunter made his way unsteadily back to the table and as he sat down, Ken picked up his glass followed by Nancy.

"Toast, Hunter!" Ken announced.

"Sure, Ken – what are we toasting?" Hunter asked.

"You, Hunter. We want to toast you; in our culture after spending time with us, we want you to die and then we want you to be born again."

Hunter was surprised at this; he had never heard of it before.

"So when I'm born again, can I be a little bit taller than I am?"

"Hunter, when you are reborn, you can be anything you want to be." Ken smiled as the three of them downed the hooch in one go!

Hunter knew immediately that he had been given some sort of substance as his whole body suddenly froze stiff and he began to panic.

Nancy moved next to him and gently stroked his back.

"Don't fight it, Hunter. Just relax – this is what you need; we are going to take care of you."

Hunter had experienced a 'Mickey Finney' before; somebody had slipped an LSD tablet into his drink and this feeling was similar.

Ken spoke directly to him.

"You said you wanted Indian healing, Hunter. Well, this is it. You will die, and then you will be reborn. I'll see you on the other side."

Hunter was completely paralysed. He was aware of his surroundings but it was like an out of body experience; he was looking down on himself. He watched as the big Ken picked up his small limp body and took him to the tepee at the back of the house. Then he watched Winter stop playing with the children and howl the big wolf howl, when she saw him in such a state.

The flap to the tepee opened as Ken placed Hunter inside before stopping her coming in.

She was going frantic until two elder statesmen Indians arrived and sat cross-legged a little way back from the tepee, before calling to her. She calmed and laid herself on the ground, staring into their eyes and sitting with them for the next four hours.

The children all gathered around sitting outside the tepee, led by Nancy.

Eventually Ken came out and joined everyone at the head of the semi-circle of people outside.

They began to chant before more Indians arrived and formed another semi-circle of people, then another and another. It seemed like the whole tribe had turned up for this event.

Drums had been beating for a while but now they suddenly stopped as the now two hundred strong congregation began to sing the healing song – beautiful harmonies filled the air as they all sang.

Hunter saw this all before his mind was whisked into the tent to become one with his body once again.

Inside the tepee, Hunter felt the hot steam around him and immediately began to sweat profusely.

He had been laid on a bed of spruce and sniffed at the comforting smell of pine trees beginning to relax. 'Do nothing', 'say nothing', 'be nothing', he thought as his training had taught him, but this time it seemed impossible to get inside of himself, especially as two very attractive Indian girls naked from the waist up were beginning to undress him. Thankfully they didn't cut his clothes away this time; just gently removed everything and folded them neatly before placing them to one side.

They then began to clean him from top to bottom removing his dressings from his chest and belly, then his half amputated big toe. This they took great care in doing looking at the still festered red stump and communicating silently between themselves. Every so often, one would hold Hunter's head up and the other would make him drink a healing brew.

All the time they were feeding the small fire in the middle of the tent. The flames heated the stones that would create herbal-infused red-hot steam, when the secret brew was added.

Hunter in his semi-conscious state began to dream strange dreams, mostly about Vietnam and the people he had killed; this made him begin to fear for the first time in his life. Perhaps all the dead souls were coming to get him and he was now vulnerable and unarmed. He attempted to move but was still paralysed and could barely blink, let alone move.

The girls then began to massage his head and worked on his long straggly grey hair which they combed before tying a pony tail. He was still wearing his Indian headband and Niki produced a beautiful eagle feather and attached it upside down.

One of the girls then produced a cutthroat razor which caused another bad memory to appear.

Niki held his head firm as Rebecca shaved off his sparse grey beard from his round face before looking at her work.

"He really does look a little bit like Geronimo," she giggled and Niki nodded in agreement.

These words echoed in Hunter's spaced-out mind.

"Looks a bit like Geronimo, looks a bit like Geronimo, looks a bit like Geronimo!"

Thoughts of his dear friend, Mickey came flooding back but then they soured as the ghost of his friend began shouting abuse at him. They had always verbally abused each other but this was different; Mickey was shouting pure venom at him and Hunter suddenly became confused and hurt. Tears began to roll down his cheeks and as the girls wiped them away, they nodded at each other – the healing was working.

They then worked on Hunter's shoulders and still limp arms, massaging them with spruce mixed with herbs; he could feel the effect but couldn't move.

Niki then ran her fingers around the outsides of Hunter's chest wounds as Rebecca fussed around a pot of hot clay which she brought closer to the patient. Using wooden spoons, they laid the mixture onto the first open scar which caused Hunter's body to shake with pain.

Niki whispered into Hunter's ear.

"We need to do this, Hunter, so you just go away for a little while and come back when we've finished eh, there's a good boy."

Niki and Rebecca laid their hands over Hunter and began to chant a prayer that sent him right back to his childhood many years before. The term boy took Hunter right back to his younger years.

He was now with his father in Arizona being taught how to shoot a gun for the first time; he was seven years old, aiming an old Winchester repeater at a target a hundred yards away.

He held the gun loosely, the stock was an inch away from his shoulder and as he fired the thing, it came back at such a force it made him cry.

"That's your first lesson junior; see when you fire a rifle you've got to hold it tight in! I mean tight in! Then you ride the shot like a boxer rides a punch, that way it won't hurt."

His father had also noticed that Hunter had hit the target right in the middle.

"Good shot though, Junior, try it again, correctly this time."

The young Hunter then reloaded the weapon and shot five times more in quick succession, obliterating the small target area even though he had broken his young collar bone on the first shot. His decision to ignore the pain would stand him in good stead for what he was going to experience in later life.

"Good job, boy! Damned good job! You can now go out and find us our next meal!"

Hunter's father had joked before taking Hunter home and had even put his arm around his son in a rare show of affection.

They got back to their house in the Arizona desert and the father was shouting his praises towards his mother as they walked into the house.

Hunter had got so excited at the praise being heaped on him that he had forgotten about the step up into the house and stubbed his right toe straight into the concrete step causing him to jump around on one foot. Some pain you just can't ignore.

"Junior, you are a natural shooter, but you are a clumsy little kid."

His father had said to him and now the word, "Kid, Kid, Kid," echoed in Hunter's mind as he awoke to the same pain as his stubbed toe, to watch Niki and Rebecca covering his foot with the hot clay potion.

He felt little weights of clay on his chest and stomach and struggled to look down at them.

The girls sensed that he had come back to them and went to the next healing stage.

Outside, even more Indians had arrived. Before Hunter had drifted away temporarily, Niki had indicated to them for a lull in the proceedings, and the tribe had set up camp fires and were having a rare Yankton Sioux gathering. This had been for two hours, even though in Hunter's mind, it might have been two seconds.

All the time, the two elders had sat with Winter and communicated with her.

"You know this, man?"

"He's all I have – he's all I can trust."

"Why did you save his life?"

"I needed him."

That was as far as they could both go with her. Winter despised human conversation with all her soul. Don't talk about it, just do it.

Ken brought her over, one of the rabbits that Burt and her had hunted that day,

Ken had skinned the small animal and held it out to her.

She sniffed at the meal before taking it from Ken's hand.

Ken then backed away, letting her rip into the small animal.

A signal came from Rebecca in the tepee.

Ken shouted out a command and the whole tribe once again gathered around and began to sing the healing song, this time with four hundred or more Indians singing. It was a powerful tune and Hunter heard it clearly through the walls of the tepee. He had been through death and fear, the next task was love, unknown to Niki and Rebecca, this was Hunter's greatest fear. To actually be in love with someone and have the responsibility of looking after them was too much. He would have to lock them away in case even the smallest thing happened to them.

"What do you love, Hunter?" Niki shouted into his ear.

Hunter fought long and hard with this question – *what is love? What is anything? I am Hunter and the world is the world according to me.*

"Love is love, Hunter," the girls said as they knelt on either side of his head, holding hands and chanting until he suddenly felt power in his arms and reached out aggressively. They grabbed hold of an arm each and struggled to hold him down.

"Anger is his love, Niki!" Rebecca shouted.

"Who do you love when you kill, Hunter?" Niki asked loudly which calmed Hunter in his prone state and he laid there for the next two hours thinking about this question in his out of state mind. It was the opposite of everything normal; you shouldn't love when you kill, but he was the opposite of everything normal – anger made him calm and then he finally mixed the words in the question around in his mind and came up with,

"Maybe I love to kill."

He then began to struggle again until Rebecca looked out of the tepee and gave Ken a hand sign to which he replied,

"Woop, woop, woop!" Anger.

Drums began to beat and a war dance began; even Winter joined in with her natural wolf's howl and was pleased when old Burt joined her and howled alongside. The 'hey-hey' sounds of a war dance filled the air and went on for the next hour.

Hunter then began to sleep at the sound of the warlike drums and Indian chants until everyone sensed the end and they all stopped as suddenly as they had started.

Then everyone started to leave.

The two elder Indians paid their respects to the she-wolf as they got up to go and she went to join Nancy who was still sitting near the entrance to the tepee.

After a while, Niki looked to Rebecca and suggested.

"Shall we let her in?"

"Wouldn't hurt," she replied.

Niki opened the flap of the tepee and pointed to Nancy and Winter – "You two come in."

It was four o'clock in the morning; they had been healing for the past eight hours.

All the children had gone to bed, the Indians had all left after the party, ken was sitting asleep holding a glass of his home-made hooch and only Nancy and Winter were still waiting.

Winter walked into the tepee feeling the heat from the small fire, now calmed from what it had been.

She sat upright next to Hunter and pawed at his face.

His nose gave a little sniff, the same as it had done back in Canada when they had first met; she sniffed back at him and was assured.

Winter glared at the two sisters as they both dressed themselves and sensed some connection with them; they had looked into Hunter's soul and now knew him the same way as she did.

She then turned to Nancy and looked into her eyes communicating once again.

"I am indeed in a strange world; the things you do, the things you say I will never understand."

"When he awakes, he will be re-born and if you like honey child, you can be his mother."

She spoke to Winter who looked confused again and just glared back at Nancy for a few minutes before the woman left her and Hunter alone together...

"You are wrong, human – I am already his mother!"

***

Hunter awoke two hours later and the first thing he saw was Winter's sleeping face next to his, snoring a wolf snore.

It was still warm in the tepee and as he sat upright still completely naked; he felt the clay dressings drop from his chest. He picked off the two now-dried-out pieces of clay from his stomach and put them to one side before looking down to his foot with the heavy clay dressing.

He shook his foot but this wasn't coming off any time soon.

He then spotted his borrowed biker clothes neatly folded at once side of the huge tent and gently moved away from the still-sleeping wolf to dress himself. The clay dressing on his foot only just fitted through the leg of his jeans but then he managed to dress himself with the rest of his clothes, and it was only when he went to put on a tee shirt, that he realised that his chest and belly wounds were now pain free. He felt his hands over the crusty scars and felt no pain at all.

She awoke and as usual laid on her back to stretch out her legs and yawned.

"Hey girl, what happened here? Did I just have some Indian healing or something?"

"Apparently so!"

"Well, something has worked, so you have to respect that, eh?"

"Oh, whoopy doo!"

Hunter rounded on her and pointed a finger.

"Did you just say whoopy do – you did, didn't you? I heard it! You have to have a little more respect for these people, girl!"

"Yes, well and apparently, I am your new mother!"

"Oh man, I need a cigarette and a cup of coffee."

"I need to run in the forest."

"See you later, girl."

"Meet with you later, human."

Hunter opened up the zipped entrance to the tepee and Winter bounded off into the forest as he limped back into the kitchen, dragging his clay bound foot with him and carrying his spare boot and sock.

Hunter stoked up the wooden-fed stove and put on the coffee pot. His packet of cigarettes was still on the table and he lit one up feeling that everyone in the house was still asleep.

Sipping at a cup of stale but hot coffee, he began to think again before a familiar sound distracted him, Harleys! Hunter went outside and watched as five bikes came down the hill towards Ken's houses followed by the fridge wagon, noticing that somebody had replaced the front bumper with a four-foot length of industrial steel welded to the front of the vehicle.

Jez was the first to greet Hunter and picked him up in a huge bear hug but unfortunately stood on his foot as he put him down causing the clay to shatter and Hunter to jump around on one leg before he realised that there was no pain from his foot.

Jez began to apologise but Hunter just smiled at him pointing to his foot.

"No pain, Jez. I've been healed man! I've died and gone to heaven, then I've come back for a cup of coffee. How good are you guys – nice to see you all by the way."

Doc ran over to inspect Hunter's toe and was visibly amazed.

"That shouldn't have happened, but it has happened."

"Yea check this out, Junior," Hunter said raising his tee shirt to show the Doc his crusty but almost-healed chest and belly wounds.

Doc looked suspiciously at his ex-patient and for a final check opened up his ever-present doctors' leather case and thrust a thermometer into Hunter's mouth.

Hunter chewed at it and danced around stupidly for a half minute before the Doc pulled it out of his mouth and inspected the reading.

"Normal, Hunter. I guess I have to bow down to Indian Healing; my five years of medical college pails into nothing alongside this."

"Hey don't put yourself down, Junior – you kept me alive long enough for me to get here, remember."

They all began walking back to the Kitchen before Hunter suddenly stopped and questioned Jez.

"Hey, Jez, what the hell it that all about?" pointing at the fridge wagon.

Jez smiled back and replied.

"We have a plan – Hunter, oh boy do we have a plan!"

***

At Ma's place the monotony had been going on day after day. Thankfully they had stopped sedating her and she had calmed right back into her kind, little, old lady mode just after Hunter's brief call. She had indeed recognised his voice and she knew he was coming to get her. The arrival of Steven had broken the boredom and they had checked him out from top to bottom.

Hunter had no connections with motorcycle clubs and Ma had cleverly compounded this when they told her that Steven was not her Mickey; he was a random bikerthat had lost his way.

She had then ranted on about the Hell's Angels and how Mickey and Hunter despised them, even quoting Hunter, "If they wanted to wear a uniform, they should have joined the army!"

Even so they had attached a short-range tracking device to Steven's bike and watched him leave North Dakota from their communications room' which had been set up in Mickey's old bedroom.

The picture on the bedside table had not been missed and so now they had a small idea of what Hunter looked like.

If they connected Steven to 'Sweet Home Chicargo' and found the sniff of a wolf being there, then they would have a trail, a big one, and it was only a matter of time before that happened.

Steven had been correct in his observation of the men at Ma's house; they were indeed all old and all ex-FBI. The manager of the project was a personal friend of Hans Schnell.

Tom Preacher had been very fond of Helga and had always wondered why she was with that selfish, Swiss bastard – Hans Schnell. Even so, at the news of her unfortunate death, he had offered his services straight away and Hans had gratefully accepted.

After the debacle with the Chippewa Indians, Hans had begged Tom Preacher to come out of retirement for one last project and so he had gathered his old friends together.

He still had links to serving FBI friends and gaining information was not a problem. He himself had questioned Ma over and over about Mickey, Hunter and the wolf and the more he heard, the less he liked this project. He now knew that Mickey and Hunter were ex-special forces and had been shocked by the size of Mickey's personal arsenal laid out in the basement.

He was unsure about whether to have it all taken away or to leave it as evidence in the case of something brutal happening and after all he was surrounded by old but highly trained ex-agents.

Even though they had not been field agents and had mostly spent their time looking for international tax evasion whilst sat at desks, one little ex-special forces guy and a wolf shouldn't have been much of a problem.

Tom Preacher had also decided to use some of the basement weapons so that they were well-armed and were prepared for any sort of intrusive attack or rescue mission.

Secretly embarrassed at the way he was being used, he could sense that something was wrong and that a storm was coming his way, so he kept his well-paid team on their toes – all twelve of them.

***

Ken walked downstairs into the kitchen, very hungover and greeted Jez in a brotherly hug before turning to look at Hunter who spoke first.

"Hey look at you, Ken. Surely, I should look like you right now and you should look like me!"

Hunter shouted excitedly.

Ken stared at him with wide eyes maybe somewhat red and replied,

"Welcome back, Hunter – you surely are reborn!"

"I surely am, Ken, but I have one question."

"Fire away, Hunter."

"Who ate the placenta? Did you have that? Bet you gave it all to her, didn't ya?"

Hunter asked carrying on his bad joke relationship with Ken.

Doc had to explain to a couple of the bikers what placenta was but it was too early in the morning for bad jokes so they just got down to business.

Jez produced the diagram of Ma's house that Hunter had drawn out and shown to Steven. He hadn't let the young man take it with him in case things got heavy and they searched him. Jez had kept hold of it studying it, after all he was part Indian and in times of war, they were great planners.

The diagram only showed the outside of the big house and the gates into the property so all Jez could do was to plan a way in.

Hunter listened intently.

"One road, one way in, heavily guarded so the element of surprise is pretty much unachievable. Therefore, we need a show of overwhelming force to gain entry. We need them to think we are going in one way but then come in the other – are you agreed so far?"

Hunter was impressed; bad jokes were over – this was serious stuff.

He nodded in agreement.

"I take it there is another road that will take me to this position here in our newly created ramming vehicle that you see parked outside."

Jez pointed at the North end of the road leading to Ma's house and Hunter nodded knowingly already working out the route the fridge wagon would have to take to be in position.

"So we need to have them concentrating on the South end of the road so that I can steam in and ram the gates thus creating a passage into the target area so *et voila*."

Jez suddenly spoke in French before producing the lead covered tracking device.

The One Percenters liked my plan; one of their guys will cruise up and down a couple of miles away within range of their trackers and they'll think it's just Steven lost again. At a given time, he will then head straight for the target area. All their attention will be towards him on the south end of the road. When he's nearby, I will burst through the gates and the cavalry will take out the outside observers before following me in to the fort – what do you think so far, Hunter?

Hunter was indeed impressed and lit his customary cigarette before smoking it down and immediately lighting up another. After smoking his second cigarette, reckoning that the firepower would mostly come from the inside of the house, he suggested,

"When you get inside, they will rain fire down on you; had you thought about that?"

"Sure have, Hunter. You're already going to be in there and you'll take them all out before we ride in. If you'd given me a plan of the whole area then I'd have worked it all out for you so don't tell me that you don't know a back way in to this place."

Hunter indeed knew the whole area like the back of his hand. When he had visited Ma's place in the past, Mickey had never let his professional mind go and would go through scenarios with Hunter as they walked drunk around the fields at the back of the house and he would show Hunter the secret ways in and out of the property.

"See if my Ma's house was being attacked, I'd set this up here, and that over there; this tree would be for observer and sniper to cover the back end and if they had to retreat back to the house, you come in this way."

Mickey had lifted up an innocent-looking drain cover with a little piece of rope attached to the cover which led down some steps to a blank piece of board which he tapped on and produced a hollow sound.

"You know we are, Hunter? Do you know what's on the other side of this thin wall?"

"Four naked women waiting for sex!" Hunter had joked.

"Better that that, Hunter. This is where I keep my sexy weapons."

Hunter had always thought that this was another way into Mickey's basement and his stash of weapons.

When it came to ordinance, Mickey was a freak. He had made good friends with their camp's armourer and every time a piece of equipment had become updated, Mickey had gone home with some of the redundant stuff, which included a whole range of M16s. The claymore mine had been a one off, the guy didn't have the authority to sign off this piece of equipment but Mickey had begged him for it and paid the guys fine for his slovenly paperwork charge.

Oh yea, Hunter knew how to get into the house and then he got it – the anomaly that he was looking for.

The upper windows looked down to the side of the house where the main open area was; if the cavalry came in line astern and stayed close to the house, then they would escape the arc of fire from the upstairs windows, where he imagined the main shooters would be based. The old house had been modified over the years and above the porch leading into the house was just one small window in the attic – that was their problem – they would have to deal with that; he couldn't be in two places at one time.

He guessed that Ma would either be in the kitchen or in her own room on the first floor. He would have to point this out.

Hunter then requested another piece of paper from Ken and drew out the whole area; the missing bits of the map for Jez and told them where he would be and what he would do. Ma would be inside of the house and protected once they began the attack. He was sure of that but he would wear his cowboy weapon for any eventual stand-off thinking of Clint Eastwood shooting the bad guys straight through the head as they held their hostage.

Hunter sat back, arms behind his head enjoying the fact that he was back in the day and planning a new mission with keen people that were all on his side. Then he caught the eye of Ken and Nancy who had just come down to the kitchen. The three of them walked outside for a private conversation.

Hunter stood silently looking at his new friends knowing that he would have to leave soon and never come back.

"Guys, I know what you are going to say so let's just have a hug eh."

"No, Hunter, you don't know what we're about to say," Nancy announced seriously.

Hunter took a step back and looked at them seriously. This time his new friends were not joking.

Ken spoke,

"When you finally leave here, you will never come back. You are a marked man and you will be tracked down and killed. Nancy's sisters saw this – she can stay and we will protect her. I promise you that but who knows who is coming after you. I can't put our family in that line of fire, my friend."

Hunter knew they were right; they would be tracking him and not the wolf – she could just disappear anytime she liked, as long as they were together then the focus would be on him.

"Hey, Ken, I perfectly understand; as soon as I get Ma, we'll be on our way. She can stay here if she likes; she's her own person and I'll let her decide that when the time comes, but could you put Ma up too? Her and Winter are like kin."

"Who's Winter, Hunter?" Nancy asked slightly confused.

"Oh sorry, guys, I never made formal introductions to you. It's her in the forest, my wolf friend – we call her Winter, well Ma does anyhow, I just call her wolf."

"Or girl," Nancy said smiling.

"Yea anyhow, she love's this place and it is Ma's dream to retire by a lake and a forest just like it is here – can you guys accommodate that? I have money – we can build a new house and all."

Nancy didn't even look at her husband for agreement.

"We thought that already, Hunter – it's only you that has to go."

Hunter smiled back and shook her hand first then, as he took Kens hand, he proposed a bet.

"Bet you twenty bucks I come back, Ken."

"That's twenty bucks I hope I loose, Hunter."

Two more Harleys then drove down to the house. Hunter didn't recognise them but thought they maybe something to do with Jez's One Percenter friends. They were also not allowed onto the reservation but Hunter guessed that these guys could go anywhere they wanted to.

Parking up close to the three of them who were quickly joined by Jez, the two bikers took off their sunglasses and Hunter was pretty amazed at one of them who wasn't much bigger than himself. The small guy walked towards them with a friendly smile followed by huge biker, even bigger than Jez.

"Hi Ken, hi Nancy," the little guy said shaking hands with the couple as Hunter watched noticing that Ken did not smile back at him. He then nodded a greeting to Jez.

"And you must be Hunter. I'm so pleased to make your acquaintance – my name is Rory."

He said in an exceptionally polite fashion before grabbing Hunter's hand squeezing an extremely firm handshake.

"Likewise, Rory," Hunter replied, not relenting at the little guy's strength in his hand.

He was not what Hunter had expected as the president of a Hell's Angels' chapter and found himself to be quietly impressed by his manner, being such a small guy. Hunter normally put people off their guard by acting the idiot but this little man demanded respect straight away.

"I think we have some business to discuss?" Rory asked looking towards the house.

"Coffee is on Rory. Yours is black with two brown sugars, I remember?" Nancy said ushering everyone into the kitchen.

"It sure is Ma'am. How kind of you to remember," Rory replied eloquently as they headed into the kitchen and all gathered around the large table.

Jez produced the now two diagrams of the target area and Rory listened intently at Jez's half of the plan before turning to Hunter.

"What do you think, Hunter. You are the professional here and you have local knowledge which puts us all in your capable hands," Rory answered suspiciously.

Hunter had indeed been impressed by Jez's big entrance plan but there was much more work to do.

"This is good," he spoke running his finger over the entrance route but then pointed to the area at the side of the house.

"This is bad; they will fire from these upper windows but if you keep close to the house, you are out of their arc of fire. The one window here, however, he pointed to the attic window above the porch, you have to cover on your way in. By the time that you are outside the property, I will be inside the house."

"None of you come in – just deal with what's outside and I will deal with what's inside." Hunter advised seriously.

"You are approaching from the rear I take it Hunter; there is a small matter of surprise involved here – you will need stealth and cunning – our timing must be impeccable. Can we trust you to be in position before we make our cavalry charge into the area?"

Rory asked looking into Hunter's eyes.

"You have to trust me, I have a good partner."

"Who's your partner?"

"She's sitting right behind you."

Rory turned around and stared straight into Winter's eyes who had arrived silently and sat down hearing the whole plan.

Even this little controlled man showed his vulnerability as he looked at her. She began to growl aggressively at him, not really liking what she could feel.

"Well, Hunter, it appears that we have a reasonable plan to rescue this little, old lady; she must be precious to you?" Rory asked after gaining his composure.

"She sure is dude."

"When is it going to happen?"

"Within the next two days."

"What exactly is in this project for us?" Rory asked, getting to the nitty gritty.

Hunter thought for a while trying to recall all the weapons in Mickey's cellar.

"M16s mostly, at least five AK47s, box of grenades, 9 mm pistols, probably 12 or more, all with ammunition, a unique selection of antique and modern shotguns – the list could go on and on and somewhere there is a stash of Semtex with fuses, but I'm going to need that when we're done. I have to bring closure down on this house."

"Be like the fourth of July," Rory said excitedly.

"More like the end of one of my worlds," Hunter said profoundly.

"I'll await Jez's call and we'll work on the timing; nice to meet you again, Hunter. I hope next time we will meet under different circumstances. I really do hate violence you know."

Rory spoke and the young Doc audibly choked on his coffee.

Rory put his hand on Doc's shoulder which made him visibly nervous.

"Be sure you're wearing you're Red Cross armband Doc, wouldn't want you to be hit by friendly fire now would we?"

Winter fired a warning growl at him as he left the bench sensing some menace.

"My, my, you are an exceptionally unfriendly doggy," Rory said condescendingly causing her to rise up and give him a full-blown wolf warning snarl.

"Winter!" Nancy called to her and was amazed when this word silenced her snarling, but she still held Rory's stare.

"He's on our side," she explained.

"You are wrong, human – he is on his side."

Rory smiled again and clicked his fingers at his enormous companion who got up at this command, then merely waved at the people around the table.

The two One Percenters then left in a loud roar of Harley Davidson sounds.

Jez and his few men were desperate for a drink in their excitement so Ken produced yet another jug of his home-made hooch. Hunter picked up another cup of coffee and went out to the VW once again to meticulously clean his weapons.

Nancy fed Winter and old Burt before she leapt over Hunter to sleep on her bunk, careful not to step on any of his weapon components that he had carefully laid out.

Ken joined him sitting cross-legged on the ground, smoking an Indian peace pipe.

"Have some of this, Hunter," Ken spoke holding the pipe towards Hunter who knew the significance and stopped working for a while.

Hunter pulled a drag on the herbal tobacco and handed the pipe back to Ken.

"Thanks, Ken. I mean it; thank you so much for what you and Nancy have done for me and my girl. I never asked for any of this but I guess it's karma. I should had died a hundred times in Vietnam but never got a scratch, so if it does happen like your girls said it will then, I'll be killed a happy man!"

Ken smiled and handed the pipe back to Hunter after taking another drag himself.

"Anything else we can do for you, Hunter?"

Hunter thought for a second before asking Ken something he had been thinking about.

"Ken, this may be a stupid, stupid question, but do you have a bow with arrows that I could borrow?"

"Hunter, you kill me man; you are asking an Indian if he has a bow and arrows?" Ken answered laughing.

"I need to sneak up on someone."

"What! Just like an Indian?"

"Well, I ain't fighting General Custer, you bucket head!"

"I have the perfect weapon for you, Hunter – can you shoot?"

"Of course, I can't shoot. I'm Apache remember – we only hunted and killed with stolen US Army Winchesters; before that we threw rocks at buffalo and caught alligators from swamps with our bare hands."

Ken descended into a fit of laughter; he loved Hunter's sense of humour – it was the same as his own.

The pipe was finished and Ken got up somewhat unsteadily.

"Hunter, I need to sleep some more, then I'll show you how to use my pride and joy."

"Sure thing, Ken – love you man."

Hunter carried on cleaning his weapons, listening to the sound of laughter from Jez and his boys in the kitchen. How he would love to have joined them but, in his world, the party was always after the event. Never before.

***

Back in North Dakota, Ma was making coffee for the ex-FBI agents, acting her usual 'gentle, old lady self'. Being the wise, old bird that she was, she had stopped drinking her favourite tipple – Woodford Reserve American whiskey because she knew too much would let her mouth run riot on these people and she would give away too much information. She wasn't Mickey's mum for nothing and even though Hunter had chastised him so much, he had been a very capable killer, even more so than Hunter.

Her encounter with the Chippewa Indians had obviously not been logged down maybe because of their macho attitude and pride; they didn't want anyone to know that a little, old lady had got the best of them. Ma had fought and screamed when Tom Preacher and his team had first arrived before realising what she was up against, all on her own. She just hunkered down into her own self with Mickey and Hunter's advice that they used to say together ringing in her ears.

"'Do nothing', 'say nothing', 'be nothing'."

This had been before they drugged her up and began their interrogation. She went into a complete shell and steadfastly refused her mind to go anywhere else but the fact that she was a little, old lady all alone, waiting for her son to come home from the war.

"When my Mickey comes back, he's going to kick all your arses."

was the most aggressive thing she had said in the previous three weeks and this one comment had made Tom Preacher really think about this particular project.

Mickey was already dead, Hunter Wisekat was at large in America with a killer wolf, and he was under orders from an arrogant Swiss bastard who wanted him to wait where he was, using an old lady as bait.

Tom Preacher did not like where he was at this time. He lived in a beautiful house with a large pension mostly spending his time, writing his memoirs.

Just like the wolf hound dog before him, he just wanted to get up the next morning and run away. He could sense the danger. But he couldn't walk away on this occasion – his team relied on him.

***

A couple of hours later, Hunter was cleaning the Colt45, the cowboy gun that he hated probably because the off-white mother of pearl handle reminded him so much of General George S Patton of WWII fame.

"Arsehole!" Hunter would mutter every time he touched the thing.

It wasn't that he couldn't use it; he knew he could have taken out the Indian and his wolf hound back in Wisconsin in less than a second, even with a dislocated shoulder but one of the innocent bear hunters had been pointing a weapon at him and he would have had to kill him as well. Mickey would have killed all of them.

Hunter hated senior management with such a desire and his thoughts turned to Rory who was probably the equivalent of everything he despised about his army life. He was the man in charge and would have to be at the very sharp and pointy end of this project to gain any respect from him.

His personal thoughts were suddenly interrupted by the thud of an arrow landing just a few inches from his foot. Winter was awake in a second and stood beside Hunter snarling at the threat in front of her and her dragon human.

Hunter calmed her down in a second.

"It's OK, girl – they're just having fun."

Hunter spoke seeing Ken with a bow in his hand and Jez with the other bikers laughing like apes but then they all stopped, seeing the response from Winter.

"Fun? What is fun? Wake me up again at your peril, humans."

She then went back to her bunk and sighed heavily before sleeping again.

Ken then walked towards Hunter apologising as he did.

"Sorry, Hunter! I have to keep my hand in."

"Sure thing, Ken," Hunter answered smiling, taking the sheath of arrows from him and slinging them over his back.

He then looked for a target and noticed a wooden carved weather cock that was swaying in the gentle breeze on top of the house maybe 40 yards away from where he was and held his hand out to receive the bow.

"Oh no! Not my weather cock! My uncle made that for me!"

Hunter fired off three quick shots, spinning the thing around and it ended with three arrows sticking through the beautifully crafted structure, all grouped together.

Ken was in awe and the rest of the bikers went quietly back to their drinks knowingly.

"What can't you kill with, Hunter?" Ken asked seriously.

"Well, Ken, I met up with a British special forces guy once who told me he had taken out somebody with a copy of the New York Times, so I guess I'm still learning."

"That's not a joke, is it?"

Hunter just shook his head – it wasn't a joke.

"Nancy told me that her sisters asked you a question that you could not answer during the healing. It was 'Who do you love, when you kill?'"

Hunter thought for a while at this question which again reached into his soul and decided to stop the conversation there and then.

"I have only ever killed bad guys, Ken and hey, your bow is great! Can I borrow it for a short time? I promise to bring it back, either that or it will go out in a blaze of glory. It's a great bow man!"

Ken walked back to the kitchen and produced yet another jug of homemade hooch; it was almost his last one but he thought the occasion deserved it.

***

Later that day Hunter fired up the VW and beckoned Winter inside.

"What! why do we have to leave this place? It's wonderful!"

"We have to go get Ma."

On hearing the word 'Ma', Winter jumped immediately on to the passenger seat and scratched around as usual making herself comfortable.

"Well, I do hope we are coming back here, I will kill you if we don't."

"Yea I'm sure you'll kill me if we don't come back here, girl."

Four hours later, Hunter parked the VW about a mile away from Ma's house and dressed himself for war. It was 4 am. And the air was still but mild.

The Dragunov remained under his bunk; it wouldn't be much use in this tight, enclosed area so he just took the huge long sights and Mickey's M16A1. He strapped the cowboy weapon to his right thigh, fixed his hunting knife in position at the small of his back and put on the canvas bag that he had taken from Richard1.

Alongside the money in the bag, he had also found a couple of tins of camouflage paint and began dressing his face with brown and green stripes which this time he likened to war paint and boy, was he on the warpath.

Winter looked at him and her blood also began to boil as her locked up memory appeared once again.

"Man in the forest, dressed as the forest," she was also on the warpath.

He finally strapped the M16A1 on his back and just carried the bow and sheath of arrows; he wouldn't need them once inside the house and couldn't afford to be too cluttered up with weapons.

He and Winter carried on from where they had left off from the huge Nicolet forest. This time moving a lot slower and in much less pain but stopping regularly to let her sniff out for danger.

They moved stealthily through an old apple orchard; the grass had been allowed to grow around the trees which provided ample cover for the unlikely couple. They edged closer for the next hour until they reached their first objective, just as Mickey had pointed out to him years before. A hundred yards from the outer fence was a huge old oak tree. In the dark, Hunter could see that they had lent a ladder up towards the large branches that acted like a natural watchtower. Winter sniffed excitedly confirming Hunter's thought – there were two men in the tree.

They took cover behind the last of the big, old overgrown apple trees, its branches hanging down and meeting with the long grass. Hunter then, without even thinking about it, pointed his index finger at her, "You," then he wiggled two fingers, "walk!" – finally he made a circular motion with one finger – "around," before pointing to his nose and sniffing gently.

She was off in a split second and skirted the whole area before coming back to him, fifteen minutes later.

As she arrived by his side, he held out one arm. Had she bitten into it, then he would have known there was something else that she wanted to show him but she just ignored it and sat facing the danger.

Hunter then waited, listening intently before he heard the sound that he was waiting for.

Two clicks. This was an hourly radio check without speech. Someone inside the house would press their transmitter button for a second and the receiving party would reply by doing the same, barely exchanging communications but ensuring they were still in touch.

Hunter checked his watch – it was bang on 6 am. The biker with the tracking device would uncover it from its lead casing at 6:45 am and begin the subterfuge, two miles away from the house. He reckoned that there would be a small commotion when they picked up the signal and would alert the people inside and outside, if they did indeed pick it up and point their attention to that direction.

After the expected radio check at 7:00 am, he would remove the rear-guard threat and make his way into the house, giving himself 30 minutes to take out the combatants inside before Jez would burst through the outer gates at 7:30 am, which was calculated to be first light.

In theory, the plan was good but as with all plans, they are subject to change and Hunter had calculated at least five other options and so readied himself with Ken's bow as 6:45 am approached.

At 6:47 am, the radio in the tree suddenly clicked four frantic clicks – warning. Hunter moved into the open and silently shot the first shadowy figure holding a pair of binoculars in the chest; the other who was replying with the button on the radio stupidly looked towards Hunter who put the next arrow straight into his forehead.

"CONTACT! We have a contact!" the agent in Mickey's old bedroom shouted if only to relieve the boredom that they had all suffered during the previous three weeks. Tom Preacher had been asleep in the kitchen and burst into the room to look at the vague tracking screen.

"Which one?" he asked. They had attached a half dozen tracking devices to anyone who had stopped in their area, mostly delivery drivers.

The operator looked at the screen. Every tracking device carried a unique signal so they could tell which one it was.

"Young biker guy," the operator answered.

"Is he lost again?" Tom Preacher asked.

"Seems to be. He's just driving up and down and, oh now he's just changed direction – he's heading here."

"FULL ALERT EVERYONE!"

Hunter had discussed this tactic in length with Jez; when the element of surprise is impossible to achieve, then you have to scare your opponents into submission. They know you are there, but they don't know exactly where you are until your overwhelming force comes crashing down on them. Good old Indian tactics. Build the fear, make them make the mistakes.

"Have you alerted the rear guard?" Tom Preacher asked.

"Yes sir, sent four clicks and they responded."

Hunter had got lucky; the agent in the tree had just pressed the button on his transmitter for the fourth time before the arrow thudded into his head. Hunter had quickly climbed the ladder to the huge lower branches of the tree to ensure they were both dead – they were.

He and Winter entered Ma's property through two pieces of six-foot fence that Mickey had only attached to the top cross beam. They swivelled as Hunter pushed them to one side allowing Winter to enter and then followed quickly. He still carried the bow and sheath of arrows but then put them to one side as they reached the far end of the house where Mickey's secret entrance laid. Hunter made a small circle with his hand towards Winter and she checked out the immediate area not going too far. All clear.

Hunter cleared away a pile of leaves that covered the heavy iron drain cover leading into Mickey's cellar. Picking up the piece of rope that was attached to the cover's opening handle, he pulled at it but the thing snapped straight away, rotten after all these years. Hunter struggled with the knotted end of the rope still attached to the drain cover but couldn't quite get the purchase to lift the heavy thing with just his fingers.

"Get out of my way, human," Winter shouted silently grasping the knot with her teeth and picking up the cover just enough for hunter to get his hands underneath the large piece of iron and move it to one side.

Hunter checked his watch. It was 7:07 am – there was still enough time.

They made their way down to steep concrete steps into a very small square area and Hunter pulled out his hunting knife. He made a small whole into the thin board into what Hunter deemed to be Mickey's basement armoury. The sharp knife cut an entrance into yet another small area, the place where he kept all his sexy weapons.

Hunter had made a mistake. In the now first light, all he could make out were racks of shoulder held rocket launchers, at least twenty of them. He prodded at the walls but they were all brick built. Winter suddenly started scratching at the lower area and Hunter joined in the dig. They were in the original fireplace to the house and after ten minutes of digging and smashing at the partition, they made their way into Mickey's cellar arsenal.

For Hunter, it was ten minutes too long and to add injury to hurt Hunter found that the door leading into the house was inaccessible. John Preacher had put a padlock on the cellar door.

He couldn't get into the house and Jez's entry was only three minutes away. "Hey, girl! Now we go to plan Z."

"Oh. Human just let me in and I will do everything."

Hunter stopped and looked at her and then at his watch. It was 7:30 am and as Jez burst through the doors of Ma's place, he fired a quick burst from the M16A1 to open up the door from Mickey's cellar and then backtracked to pick up three of Mickey's sexy weapons before taking cover on the opposite side of the house.

She was inside and he was outside.

Outside of the house, the guy in the Lincoln who loved bikes thought he could hear machines approaching. He and his partner had been given the warning of the young biker approaching and it was the guy that loved Steven's Triumph that got it first.

"That's not a Triumph, that's a Harley, or should I say, that's lots of Harleys."

He got out his gun and his partner did the same feeling confused. They had been ordered to shoot a wolf if ever one turned up but nobody had given them advice on what would happen if 30 Hell's Angels drove towards them at high speed, all fanned out across the street. As they got closer, they suddenly reverted to single file, in what seemed to the bike fan in the car, a well-rehearsed manoeuvre and he sat agog as the lead bike ridden by a small guy went past at high speed, firing a shotgun into the open window followed by four others firing, as they went by still keeping to the left of the road.

Meanwhile from the opposite direction, Jez and Doc drove the fridge wagon in the middle of the street as the bikers in single file passed them by.

The fridge wagon gathered speed until Jez guessed the correct moment and went headlong into the large gates, bursting through in a shower of wooden splinters. The wagon coughed to a sick halt, half way down the hundred-yard drive way and immediately began taking fire from the skylight window in the roof that Hunter had predicted.

Jez and Doc left the vehicle quickly and took cover behind the wagon as Rory rode in stopping at the same place and dismounting his bike. Two of his guys, however hell bent on glory, rode past them and were shot down by the agent in the roof space firing an AK47.

A biker then rode up to Rory carrying an ancient looking bazooka of WWII era. This was his plan for clearing out the shooter that Hunter had advised upon. Rory took charge of the weapon and ordered his man to load the rocket. He took aim and pulled the firing mechanism and the missile burst into life only to fizzle out in mid-air and explode harmlessly twenty yards before the house.

Rory threw the weapon to the ground in disgust before turning to Jez.

"Any other ideas, Jesmond?" Rory said in an annoyed fashion.

Hunter had been watching from the most exposed area opposite the house, behind the one and only tree that could provide cover; he had been amazed that he'd made it there unobserved and was now struggling to remember the firing procedure for a fairly modern rocket launcher.

He had fired one once on a range and now he had three more to practice on, he thought. Holding the thing in front of him and looking at the configuration, he thought he must have got it right and went to practice pulling the trigger, to which the merest touch of his finger sent the rocket flying high over the roof of the house.

All the fire from the centre windows in the house were now concentrated on him and he hunkered down behind the huge tree trunk as bullets rained left and right. He configured another rocket launcher knowing this time he had got it right and waited.

Rory had watched Hunter's negligent fire stream above the roof and decided to act.

"Hell or high water boys!" he shouted remounting his bike and revving it loudly, blew a kiss to Jez before heading at high speed towards the house followed by the rest of his fearless pack.

Hunter heard them coming and the bullets firing in his direction stopped for a split second – that was all he needed. He took quick aim at the roof to the left of him and this time fired the rocket accurately, removing the threat from the skylight window and setting the top of the house alight.

He quickly picked up the M16A1 and fired two whole magazines into the first-floor windows before quickly configuring the last rocket launcher that he fired into his old guest room. He calculated that Ma would have not been in her room along with the men firing machine guns. The whole top of the house then began to burn steadily.

Rory and his men drove around the house and the remaining agents on the first floor were called down to combat the threat at ground level. Hunter was desperate to get into the house – Winter was on her own.

Hunter had blasted the door to Mickey's cellar arsenal and she had thought about leaving the room but then her instincts told her to stay where she was. During her recuperation, she had wandered around the building in the night while Hunter and Ma were having a rare sleep and she knew every inch of the place.

Once the attack had begun, she had stayed in the shadows of Mickey's arsenal and had hidden in the secret room. Two agents had been sent to the basement when they heard Hunter blast the door open with his M16. She had watched the beams of light from their torches' hunt around in the basement before they had been called back. One went straight back but the other, a small fat guy had shouted to him, "No, there's something down here."

He had carried on his hunt and found the secret entrance.

Squeezing through the small hole with his large body, he looked up straight into the eyes of Winter. She had simply put her jaws around his neck and squeezed until he had stopped struggling before pulling at the dead weight with great strength so she could get back into the house. She walked through the now open door and waited in the stairwell of the steps leading up to the house listening to the high-pitched screaming of Ma laughing madly. "Here's my Mickey, boys! I've told ya, he's coming, he's coming to get ya!"

Tom preacher had been stunned at the level of violence so far and decided to try to reason his way out.

"You outside the house – what do you want?" he shouted.

Rory was now in his most sadistic mode.

"You inside the house, we want you to die!"

Tom preacher looked at his remaining six men; two of them were technical people. No way on this man's earth had he expected such a level of bad intent on this project.

Hunter had struggled to pull the dead fat agent's body away from the old fireplace before sensing Winter hiding at the bottom of the stairwell. He listened to the conversation upstairs as he and Winter silently climbed the stairs to the ground floor. He held the M16A1 gently pushing back the door and seeing Ma shaking in fear on a chair surrounded by the remaining agents – a couple of them were badly wounded.

"Games over, boys!" he said behind them as they all froze.

"It would be appropriate now if you would all drop your weapons, please."

Tom Preacher who was always unarmed indicated to his men to do so.

Ma spotted Winter behind Hunter and ran unsteadily towards her.

"Oh, my little hairy doggy, Winter! How are you my lovely? I've so missed you."

Tom Preacher witnessed something he had never seen before. A little, old lady and a wolf loving each other like family who had not met in a long time. At this point he thought about his own family and wondered whether or not he was on the right side or if indeed he was going to get out of this situation. His remaining men were still going to follow him but they were also pretty old and just wanted to get out.

Hunter looked at the old men in sorrow; they had been used by the man who thought everything was going to be easy. Once again, he broke the ice in his own fashion.

"Do any of you guys have a cigarette?"

To which they all replied, "No, no, we all gave up – it's bad for your health at our age."

Ma then walked past him heading for the kitchen.

"I've got some of Mickey's in there, Hunter. I'll get you a pack."

"And some whiskey, Ma! I think these fellas could do with a drop."

Ma passed the cigarettes to Hunter who lit one up from a light from one of the retired agents as they took turns to sip from a bottle of Ma's Woodford Reserve; she took a massive swig first before passing the bottle round.

"I gave up smoking but I still have my Zippo," the agent who had lit Hunter's cigarette proudly announced.

"INSIDE THE HOUSE! COME OUT AND BE KILLED, OTHERWISE WE'RE COMING IN!"

Hunter coughed once again at the old smoke and looked at the old agents who were now getting nervous, listening to the shouts from Rory who was obviously in full-psycho mode."

Ma and Winter sat cuddling on the floor sensing one more thrust of violence coming from outside – Winter began to growl.

Hunter put down the M16A1 and the canvas bag behind Winter, knowing the remaining agents would not dare approach her and walked outside the door onto the front porch to confront Rory, head on, apparently unarmed.

The little man screamed at him.

"Deal, Hunter! We had a deal! We need to get inside."

"Sure thing, Rory but there are some changes; some people are going to come out and we are going to let them live. Is that OK with you?"

Rory's boyish face had now turned into a demon-like apparatuses; he sat on his Harley with his huge second in command alongside him and the rest of the Angels behind. Hunter quickly noticed that only Rory was holding a weapon – a pump action shotgun that was now pointed directly at him.

"Damn you, Hunter, you cop lover; everybody in there is going to die!"

Just then Winter arrived at Hunter's side and began snarling viciously.

Rory glared back at her and began moving his weapon to point at her.

"INCLUDING YOUR MANGY DOG!"

In a split-second Hunter brushed aside the bottom of his jacket and drew the Cowboy Colt45 putting two bullets into the head of Rory who dropped from his bike, his finger instinctively pulling the trigger of his shotgun firing harmlessly up into the air as he fell from the bike.

Hunter flipped the handgun back into its holster in another split second and looked at the big guy who remained unmoved at the action.

"I guess you're in charge now, big fella!" Hunter shouted at him.

The big guy looked down to his ex-leader's dead body and spat before putting two fingers in his mouth and whistling loudly.

A van suddenly appeared and Hunter pointed to the back of the house where they could load up the contents of Mickey's arsenal; the fire had taken hold and there wasn't much time to get the ordinance out.

The rest of the Angels followed and they all quickly began the process of loading the weapons.

Hunter walked back into the house with Winter who went directly to Ma comforting the little, old lady who was now holding Mickey's M16 guarding the old agents.

"I assume you guys have another vehicle to get you out of here?" Hunter spoke to Tom Preacher recognising that he was in charge of their operation.

"It's in the barn," Tom Preacher spoke as smoke from the fire upstairs began to consume the downstairs.

"Send one of your guys to get it; he'll be OK, you have my word – let's get everyone outside. Is getting a bit smoky in here."

Tom Preacher sent one of his fit men to get their ride and he ran around the Angels who were franticly loading weapons into their van passing them from man to man. They all ignored him.

"I guess we underestimated you, Hunter Wisekat," Tom Preacher spoke.

Hunter just smiled hearing his name spoken through the white noise in his head. He was in no mood for a conversation with this man. In a past life, he would have taped him up and beaten him half to death to get the information he needed but he had other ideas about that. Tom Preacher was a very lucky man at this time.

Five more Harleys arrived outside the house entrance as the old agents, Ma and Winter moved to a safer place.

The agents looked worried but it was only Jez, Doc and three of their friends.

Jez and Doc had brought their bikes along in the back of the fridge wagon and were relieved to find them intact after the number of bullets, the old wagon had taken.

Doc immediately went into 'Doc mode' and began putting dressings on the seriously wounded agents to stem their flow of blood, before a large black ATV arrived from the barn. Winter was the first to react. She ran around the vehicle sniffing and growling, until another locked memory came out. Tom Preacher was helping his wounded men into the back seat and she took a huge chunk of flesh from the back of his left leg before Hunter and Ma beckoned her to calm down; they knew it was not wise to touch her in this state but their joint shouts of, "Winter!" and, "Hey Girl!" were just enough to make her think for a second. Tom Preacher managed to get into the ATV and shut the door before the vehicle sped away.

Hunter noticed the sign on the back, a red square with a white cross inside. He had also seen this vehicle before.

Ma managed to calm Winter and sat on the ground with her as she too went from being Dr Jekyll to Mr Hyde.

"Hey Ma! This is Jez, he's our friend and he's going to take you to a safe place."

Hunter shouted to her; the sound of the fire was getting louder.

Ma took one last look at her burning house and sadness overwhelmed her before she reverted to her feisty, old lady self.

"What? This big boy? On this big bike? Fire it up, son. LET'S RIDE!"

Jez smiled as he helped the little, old lady onto the pillion seat behind him; she put her hands around Jez and shouted,

"See you in a better place, Hunter, Winter – you take care of my boy!"

Ma held her hand in the air and made the 'whoop whoop' call of an Indian at war, as they sped off.

One of the Angels approached Hunter and shouted, "Hey, mister, is this what you were looking for?" throwing a small package at him, along with some arming fuses.

Hunter took the package of Semtex and wondered whether or not, it was necessary. The fire would consume everything but then his thoughts turned to Mickey. Nah, we have to go out with a bang, and this will be a big one.

Hunter took a deep breath and hurried back into the house. He picked up the M16A1 and Richard1's canvas bag into which he began to put every piece of paperwork that he could find from the communications centre, set up in

Mickey's old bedroom. Winter barked warnings at him and he eventually began to leave the house after setting the Semtex charge with a five-minute fuse, before all of a sudden, the house telephone in the kitchen rang and Hunter picked it up. Flecks of burning timber surrounded Hunter as he held the phone.

"Tom, how is everything, please give me an update," the foreign voice on the other end of the line spoke.

"Oh, Tom's not here right now, but you can leave him a message if you have anything worthwhile to say," Hunter answered cynically as Winter began growling at him furiously, telling him to get out of the burning building.

"Oh, wait a minute, here's some one here that wants to talk to you."

Hunter pointed the telephone towards her so that he could hear her franticly growling loudly – her warnings reaching fever pitch.

Hans Schnell put down the phone in his office in Switzerland – he was in shock. He had just heard the wolf that he was hunting; he heard her voice, the beast that had killed his wife – he had heard her talk.

Hunter began laughing madly as they walked out of the burning house, stopping when hot embers began landing on his head. He looked down to Winter who screamed at him as her fur was beginning to catch fire and only then he moved quickly. Outside, he patted down the fires on her long coat, realising that she was not going to leave him in there. She would have stayed with him and they would have died together.

"I'm sorry, girl. I just had a moment there – let's get out of here eh!"

"You are truly a fire dragon, why do I care so much?"

The roar of almost 30 Harley Davidsons went past them followed by a struggling van full of ordinance as the house went into its final throws. The last bike stopped with the huge and new biker president looking at them as they stood in Ma's yard for the final time.

He pointed at Hunter – "You," then at Winter – "You," – then he made the OK sign with his hand before driving off loudly.

Hunter and Winter got up and made their way out of Ma's property heading back to the VW.

"Where did that human ask us to go?"

"We're going back to your favourite place, honey. Oh my God, did I just call you honey? Why is that? Maybe I'm getting to like you."

"What is there not to like?"

Hunter picked up Ken's bow and the sheath of remaining arrows on their way back to the VW; he was happy. The mission had gone almost to plan and he had killed some more bad guys. He had also found another large stash of dollars in the communications room that he had stuffed into the really handy canvas bag once owned by Richard1 and was already thinking that maybe some of the paperwork could give him some leads towards the Swiss guy who was dogging him. He truly hated being hunted and maybe now he could revert to his natural self in name and nature – Hunter.

Most of all he was excited about seeing Ma in a safe place and getting her out of the line of fire, and now that money was not an issue, he could give her a new and better life. That would hopefully make Mickey proud of him and remove some of the demon thoughts that had been said to him during his healing experience. He would never want to go to that dark place ever again.

"Mrs Tomlin?" a small voice called from the broken outside gates of Ma's place.

"Mrs Tomlin are you o...!" *BOOM!* The Semtex device exploded and indeed the whole place lit up like the fourth of July.

***

Jez and his crew drove like the wind and they were back in South Dakota and within the safety of the reservation three and a half hours later, much quicker than Hunter and Winter would get there.

He had loved the ride with Ma, her clinging onto him and every so often he would ask her, "You OK, Ma?"

She would always respond with an arm in the air and some Indian 'whoop whoop' calls before hugging him tightly.

As the five bikes drove into Ken's place that afternoon, Jez came to a final halt.

"OK, lady – you can get off now, we are here."

Ma didn't move; she was still clutching her arms around the big guy. Jez knew something was wrong as he felt Ma's hands around him – they were cold.

"Doc, get over here," Jez shouted as the young Doc stopped his bike.

Doc took one look at Ma and knew instantly that she was dead. He went through the motions of checking for pulse or breathing but he imagined that she had died at least an hour before. Rigor mortis had already begun to set in and he got Ken and Nancy to help him remove her body from the back of Jez to get her into a respectful shape before Hunter arrived.

"Oh man, this is going to hurt him real bad," Jez observed already crying a tear for the old lady.

Everyone there cried and carried on crying until Hunter and Winter arrived two hours later.

Hunter saw the faces of the people that greeted him and Winter hurried into the house before letting out the saddest, *"Awhooooo,"* mixed with other wolf sounds that meant grief.

Doc approached Hunter who at this point just needed an explanation. The shock had caused his legs to give way and he dropped into a kneeling position.

"I'm pretty sure she had a heart attack, Hunter. She was old and maybe the …"

"OK, Junior, thank you."

"I couldn't save her."

Hunter looked up to him in desperation.

"That wasn't your job… that was mine."

"Sometimes, these things happen, Hunter."

"They tend to happen too much in my world, Doc," Hunter responded for the first time giving the young man the respect that he finally deserved before going into a dark place.

"What can we do for you, Hunter?" Doc asked worriedly.

Hunter didn't answer, he just got up and walked into the surrounding forest.

End of 'The Wolf' part one.